I0547785

SAIRA

Book V
The Illusionist Series

by

Fran Heckrotte

2016

Saira

Fifth in The Illusionist series

Copyright © 2008 by Fran Heckrotte
All rights reserved.

eBook ISBN: 978-1-939950-22-2
Print ISBN: 978-1-939950-23-9

First Edition eBook: November 2008

Publisher: Novel Ideas Publishing, LLC
Beaufort, SC. USA
Web Site: www.novelideaspublishing.com

Cover Design by Patty Henderson
Email: pattyghenderson@aol.com

Copy Editor: Cindy Burke
Email: cindyburkeoriginals@gmail.com

Acknowledgments

Thanks to all my beta readers who helped me with Saira. We have traveled on a long journey together creating The Illusionist Series. Alex D'Brassis, Lee McLean, and Kimberly, my betas...and Mary K. Bosshart, the alpha of my alpha readers.

To Pam, your help was invaluable when I first wrote this series. Thanks so much for all your hard work.

Patty G. Henderson, my cover artist. The covers are phenomenal. A work of art.

Cindy Burke, my copy editor. Great job, Cindy!

Thank you A. Lamarre. I can never really express how much you inspired me to write.

And to Howie, who is still wondering why I mention him.

CHAPTER 1

SHE WAS SAIRA, a nomad trapped in a world where space was restricted only by the limits of her imagination, and time was nothing more than a highway between the then and the now. She lived in the present only because it suited her, with no idea of her true age. Time was too irrelevant, and she was too old for it to have meaning. Saira had always existed, long before the light, long before the creation of the planets, long before the birth of the universe.

In the beginning, there was only consciousness with no spectral body. At least, that's how she remembered it. Without light, it was hard to know for sure. Then she grew aware of others and sought them out, only to become frustrated at having failed to discover their pasts or their locations. It was as if they, too, had always existed, *they* being First Born, a name Saira bestowed on them. Eventually, she accepted the futility of searching out their histories. Saira set aside her desire to discover more about them and concentrated on more attainable goals. Worlds were evolving, and with them, life...life with *threads* that connected the living to everyone in their past.

In time, population numbers spiraled upward and out of control, making it impossible to track every inhabitant. Eons

1

later, some species grew more complex and thus more interesting.

Saira was infinitely curious. It was impossible to follow everyone, so she chose only the *thread* with the strongest tug...that invisible string that tied one life to all those they had crossed and those who came before them. The *irresistible* tug raised many questions. Who owned the *thread*? Where was she being pulled to? What was happening that made one particular tug stronger than another?

Perhaps that was why she existed in the *now* rather than choosing a place in the past. The present provided her with opportunities to search all that had been, and to seek answers that explained what is. The future was a mysterious opaque window that allowed a few rays of light to pass through.

Saira knew there was something on the other side, but did not know what. She could never cross that barrier, but the past could provide insight as to what could happen. New *threads* brought new experiences and increased knowledge. As a Traveler, Saira craved knowledge.

Today, the tug came from a mortal more unique than any she had ever met, and with it came a lesson that forever changed her life and the lives of those she encountered.

CHAPTER 2

THE ILLUSION WAS almost complete. Yemaya and her team had managed to perform the ghost scenes flawlessly on the three previous nights. No one anticipated problems during the last show, but the participants remained vigilant. Mistakes happened.

The stage was a reproduction of an old cemetery. Large headstones and graves were strategically positioned around a sarcophagus. Elaborate symbols were carved into their sides. The massive lid hung from four large hooks and chains directly overhead. At each corner of the funerary box stood a torch, its flames flickering eerily in the subdued light. The smaller graves were equipped with hinged doors, allowing the *dead* to rise from the "earth" or disappear into it as the act required.

The Illusionist's method of escape was a mystery even to her crew. They had worked with her for many years. Most of them had given up trying to discover her secrets. Yemaya always supervised the details of how to stage the set. A choreographer drilled the participants until they performed their routines flawlessly. Once satisfied there would be no mistakes, Yemaya stepped in to execute her role, completing the finale. Each escape left everyone stunned, and with more questions than answers.

Compared to past performances, this particular theme was not complicated. Yemaya portrayed a frightened young woman walking nervously through a cemetery on All Hallow's Eve. Artificial fog swirled among the headstones. Gray smoky tentacles touched each object like fingers gently caressing a lover's face.

Several *corpses* milled around aimlessly while others stalked the late-night intruder. Disturbed by the presence of a live human, they closed in for the capture when she walked hesitantly around a headstone and stopped. Paralyzed by fear, the woman was unable to scream or resist clawing hands. The *dead* carried her prone body above their heads around the stage, displaying their prize to other corpses emerging from the graves. Haunting music was accompanied by a strange seductive dance. The victim's hands and feet were bound with ropes.

A few members of the audience were summoned onto the stage to examine the sarcophagus. Once they confirmed the absence of secret panels, they returned to their seats.

The ritual began. Yemaya was placed in the concrete coffin. The lid was lowered from the ceiling by a small crane. A scale attached to the crane indicated the cover weighed almost two hundred pounds. Once the tomb was sealed, a clock ticked off the seconds indicating how long a person could survive inside before suffocating. If the occupant didn't panic, five to seven minutes was the maximum limit.

At three minutes the audience grew restless. People fidgeted, looking nervously from the timer to the coffin and then back to the timer. Voices called out for the crane operator to lift the lid. Others whispered to their neighbors, sure something had gone horribly wrong. Had The Illusionist's luck finally run out? Perhaps she misjudged her abilities. Surely the frantic behavior of the participants on stage was indicative of a problem. Five minutes and the audience was on its feet yelling for the coffin to be opened.

A ghostly apparition with long white hair, pale skin and red glowing eyes appeared from offstage and whispered to two of the performers. One motioned for the crane's hooks to be lowered. After quickly attaching them to the lid, the operator slowly lifted it, moving it to the side.

The apparition reached into the coffin. Her hands swept the inside. She pulled out a black gown and showed it to the audience. Two spectators were brought back on stage to examine the sarcophagus.

"It's empty!" one shouted. "The damn thing's empty!" Glancing back inside he felt around the bottom. "And there ain't no way she got outta here through the bottom either."

Members of the audience looked around as if expecting Yemaya to magically appear next to them. When people yelled out, wanting answers, the apparition stepped to the edge of the stage and raised her arms, motioning for the crowd to quiet down.

"Ladies and gentlemen, please be seated while we figure out what has gone wrong here," she said. "Hopefully we can get to the bottom of this quickly."

She walked back to several other costumed figures who seemed to be having a serious discussion. A few nods later, the apparition returned to the edge of the stage.

"I think we have discovered what happened. The Illusionist has completed her escape from the sarcophagus. Has anyone seen anything unusual?"

"Yeah, the whole damn show!" a man yelled from one of the back rows.

"We didn't see anything," a woman near the front said more quietly.

Others nodded in agreement.

"I thought as much," the apparition replied, almost soulfully. "I guess I will have to solve this."

Reaching above her head, the ghostly figure pulled off the white wig, exposing long, raven black hair. She then peeled a thin layer of pasty white latex from her face and removed the red eye contacts. The audience gasped. Before them stood the Illusionist.

"Where'd you come from?" asked one of the men who had previously inspected the coffin.

Yemaya walked over to him and whispered in his ear. A bright red flush crept up his neck and into his cheeks. Laughing softly, she leaned down and planted a light kiss on his left cheek, ruffled his hair, and patted his back. Grinning sheepishly, he scurried back to his seat and quickly plopped down, unable to make eye contact with her or his immediate neighbors.

"What did you say to him?" a voice called out.

"I answered his question," Yemaya replied, giving the audience a wink. "I guess he was not expecting it to be quite so descriptive."

The audience laughed as vivid imaginations pictured what she must have told him. After several moments, Yemaya held up her hand and signaled for everyone to quiet down.

"Ladies and gentlemen. Tonight you have experienced an illusion, nothing more. You may think otherwise, but I can assure you, there is always a logical explanation behind everything I do. My job is to create and perform these illusions for your entertainment. Your job is to figure out how they are done. Please do not try any of these stunts, especially this one. It is extremely dangerous. My people are professionals. They are the reason I am not permanently retired." The audience laughed when she made a face while emphasizing the word *permanently* with the symbolic gesture of slicing her throat. "Once again, thank you for coming tonight. Please be safe on your way home."

Waving good-bye and walking off the stage, the Illusionist stopped next to the curtain and smiled at a young blonde woman who was frantically writing in a small notepad. Kneeling down on one knee, she remained in that position for several seconds. The audience sat quietly, waiting to see what followed.

* * *

At last, Dakota thought, unaware of the silence around her. *A pen that works. You're a keeper.*

As though she had jinxed it, the pen skipped. Exasperated, she shook it and tried again, whereupon it stopped writing completely. Dakota muttered a few swear words, stuck the tip in her mouth, and sucked hard.

Slowly, an eerie silence nudged aside her frustration. Dakota looked up, her lips puckered and cheeks drawn inward. The audience stared curiously at her. Blushing, Dakota glanced toward the stage and into pale blue eyes. The glint of humor and faint smile on Yemaya's face made her even more aware of the pen stuck in her mouth.

"Sheeyit!" She yanked it away from her lips and jammed it in her handbag. Several people chuckled. Dakota turned to glare at the offenders, then grinned sheepishly and shrugged.

This is getting annoying, she thought.

Laughing, Yemaya stood and strolled away, disappearing behind the curtains.

"You had to do it." Dakota reached into her bag for the offending pen. "You just had to stop like all the others. What is this? A conspiracy?" Disgusted, she tossed it back into her handbag and headed backstage.

"Come in," a husky voice said when Dakota knocked on the changing room door. A faint shiver travelled down her spine. "Damn," she muttered, rubbing her arms absentmindedly. Opening the door, she peeked inside.

Yemaya sat on a long couch, her legs propped across its arm and dangling. Although she looked relaxed, Dakota could tell something was bothering her. "What's up?" she asked,

7

moving quickly to kneel next to her lover and give her a brief kiss on the lips.

Yemaya frowned, unsure if she even knew. The show had gone as planned. Well, almost. After the lid was lowered onto the coffin, she remembered nothing. With the darkness of being entombed came the blackness of unconsciousness. Minutes later she found herself in her apparition costume walking onstage as if nothing had happened. The escape was a mystery to her. Not wanting to upset Dakota, she smiled and reached up to ruffle her hair.

"Nothing. I am a little tired. For some reason this show was more exhausting than normal."

"I'm not surprised. A lot goes into every performance. One of these days I'm going to figure out how you disappear and reappear like you do. I think there's more to your illusions than *illusions*."

"I have never denied that, but no one is going to believe me when I say I am an alien from another planet. Besides, sometimes I even surprise myself."

"Yeah, right. And I'm Princess Leia."

"Princess Leia?"

"You know...Star Wars."

"I never saw the movie, but I know who you mean. Carrie Fisher."

"Carrie? Geez. You sure know how to take the mystique out of things. Where's your sense of wonder?"

Raising one eyebrow, Yemaya gave Dakota *the look*.

"Cut it out," Dakota said. "Save that for your groupies."

Yemaya stood up, pulling Dakota with her, then gave her a warm hug.

"Busted. How about we get out of here? The crew will clean up. I think I could use a good night's sleep."

Dakota wrapped her arm around Yemaya's waist. She sensed something was bothering her, but didn't want to press for an explanation.

CHAPTER 3

SAIRA NEVER KNEW exactly what attracted her to the essence of another. First came the tug of a *thread*. Then she was pulled toward the entity. Whether halfway around the mortal world or a different one made no difference.

Today she was observing a young Quebecoise in a small French-Canadian community called Outrement near Montreal. The woman's energy was powerful. Following her *thread* would be interesting. Unfortunately, *that* journey had to wait.

A stronger *thread* tugged from several hundred miles to the south. Because of her ability to travel through time and space, the journey was instantaneous. She arrived at her new destination at the very moment she left the old one.

The blackness could not conceal the woman's beauty or the darkness of the *beast* dwelling within her. For now, *it* was caged in its lair, a prisoner to the will of its captor. Saira could feel it seething with frustration, biding its time, waiting to break free of the barriers holding it captive. The *beast's* essence felt vaguely familiar.

So, this is the attraction, Saira thought, reaching deep into the woman's mind to touch the darkness.

Sensing the intruder, the *beast* backed away, growled angrily, and called to its mistress. The human shifted restlessly

9

in the concrete tomb, her concentration broken by an uncomfortable feeling that she wasn't alone.

"You can feel me," Saira said, more to herself than the human.

"Yes," the woman replied. "Who are you? Why are you here?"

"All in good time, Illusionist. At the moment, you have more pressing matters. I'm afraid I've broken your concentration. You have only a few seconds to escape this place. Can you do it?"

"I have no choice," Yemaya gasped. Her breathing was labored.

Saira watched as the woman took a few deep breaths before settling into a state of deep meditation. Her heartbeat slowed. Consciousness was slipping away. The Illusionist was losing the battle...dying.

Saira waited, hoping against reason the mortal would save herself. Only after the lungs and heart stopped functioning did she intervene.

"It isn't your time," she said. The apparition had never interfered with another's life. Nothing like this had happened before. If Yemaya died now, the future would be forever altered. The ramifications could be disastrous.

After making the necessary adjustments, Saira departed, leaving the Illusionist where she needed to be, but not where she was originally.

An unexpected tug was pulling her to a new entity that had recently emerged from the Nothingness. It would be her first contact with someone from the Netherworld.

* * *

Yemaya couldn't remember how she escaped from the sarcophagus. One moment the lid was being lowered over her; the next thing she remembered was standing offstage in her apparition costume, slightly disoriented. Her assistants appeared slightly panicky, but quickly recovered when she walked onstage. Their relief was palpable. After that it was up to her to make sure the finale went as planned, even if the escape hadn't.

CHAPTER 4

ARRIVING AT HER destination, Saira found herself in a realm she rarely visited, the Underworld. Most of the inhabitants were too much alike to be interesting. The Underlord, however, was different. He was First Born. His *thread* was impossible to follow. It began at the Overworld, which could only mean one thing. Both Dis and his sibling, The Twin, originated beyond the gate. They were First Born.

Her first visit was shortly after Lilith appeared in the Underworld. The Twin's creation was unique. Dis' role in her banishment from Eden only added to Saira's fascination for the woman. He had tricked Lilith into leaving the security of Paradise simply to annoy his brother, and to satisfy his own infatuation and lust.

It was an enlightening journey, but once Lilith was with child, Saira lost interest in her. Pregnant demons were bitchy whiners who wanted nothing more than to make everyone's life as miserable as their own. There was no reason to believe Lilith would be different.

Although she was more intelligent and less volatile than the other inhabitants, Lilith was still a demoness. Dis had altered her genes, removing her human side. Understandably, as otherwise she'd never have survived in the burning heat. As a demon she could tolerate it, not to mention remain the Underlord's consort. Or so he thought.

Saira understood Lilith's craving for knowledge, but she questioned her wisdom in staying with Dis. Still, returning to the mundane existence in Paradise would have been another form of hell, only worse. She was too curious and too independent to accept a life of subservience. At least with the demons she would experience new adventures and gain the knowledge she craved. Demons and minions were dysfunctional and cantankerous and, by their very nature, teachers of life.

CHAPTER 5

THE UNDERWORLD was incredibly beautiful, vibrant and alive in a bizarre way. Brilliant flaming oranges, reds, and silver-blues contrasted with a thick billowy blackness that permeated every nook and cranny. Minor minions and demons moved stealthily among the shadows, trying to maintain their anonymity and hoping the greater demons wouldn't notice them. Each inhabitant held a unique position in the complex caste system. Upward mobility only came at the benevolence or ambition of another. There was little of the first and plenty of the latter in this realm.

The majority of residents in the Underworld spent their entire existence plotting and scheming against each other, hoping to get closer to Dis. Some sought revenge for real or imagined slights. The most wretched of his subjects focused their attentions on humanity, thus keeping his coffers filled with souls.

Souls relieved boredom. Bored minions and demons were mischievous. Dis didn't want their overly active imaginations directed at him. Idle hands literally made work for the Devil and this devil would rather satisfy his own lust than worry about *issues*.

Saira learned a lot about the Underlord during her visits. Dis wasn't very complicated, making him fairly predictable as long as he wasn't provoked.

Now, here she was again. *Why,* she didn't know, but something was about to happen to make this journey as memorable as the past ones.

* * *

Silent and invisible, Saira drifted around the preoccupied demoness who sat quietly in the overstuffed chair. Bright, wavy red hair hung loosely around her shoulders, partially concealing two small horns protruding just above the hairline. Green eyes, the color of the clearest polished emeralds, stared thoughtfully into the flames inside a hearth tucked in the corner of the dimly lit room. The index finger of her left hand tapped silently on the arm of her chair. The unconscious gesture was of one lost in thought.

She appeared to be in her early twenties, by human standards, but Saira knew this demoness was ancient. Although not First Born, her bloodline was almost as pure. Dis and the Twin's essences were strong in her, which explained the powerful tug Saira had experienced. So why, she wondered, hadn't she felt the demoness' presence before now? And why did she seem strangely familiar? Saira's musings were interrupted by a quiet but powerful voice.

"What do you want?" the demoness demanded, glancing around the room in search of the intruder. "I feel you. You don't belong here." Saira debated on whether to make her presence known or ignore the question. If she didn't answer, the demoness might decide she was just imagining her. "I know you're here. Show yourself."

Saira decided to obey the command, but only because her curiosity prevented her from leaving. She shimmered into view, settling lightly on the floor between the female demon and the fire.

"Who are you and how did you gain entry to my home without my knowledge or permission? Are you one of Father's spies?"

Cocking her head slightly, Saira smiled. First Born were always blunt, and demons were so suspicious. Apparently their offspring inherited those particular traits.

"No, and I don't need permission to be somewhere I'm not," she replied gently, not at all intimidated.

The demoness frowned. "Stop talking in riddles. You're here uninvited. Why?"

"I'm neither here nor there. I only appear to be here, therefore I need no invitation, and my purpose does not affect you, thus making the question moot."

Shaking her head in frustration, the demoness started to stand but then apparently decided against it. Instead, she settled back in her chair, crossed her legs, and assumed a nonchalant demeanor.

"I see. So now we play word games."

"I don't play games. You called to me and here I am."

"I don't even know you. Why would I call you?"

"Let's say it was your essence that beckoned to me. It's different from the others who dwell here. I was attracted to that difference. Like a moth to a flame, if I may use a human expression. You are my flame."

"Then as my moth, you're taking a big chance. Your wings could easily be singed should I desire it."

Saira laughed softly. "It's impossible to burn that which doesn't exist."

"Again the riddles. I'm not fooled. You're real enough. If you didn't exist, we wouldn't be having this interesting little chat. Unless of course I'm crazy. I assure you that isn't the case, although some would probably dispute that. Assuming I still possess a reasonable amount of sanity, who or what are you? And don't answer me with another riddle, please."

"That makes it rather difficult. How do I describe myself in a way you'll understand and not make it sound like a riddle? If I told you I don't exist in the way all things do exist, you wouldn't believe me. I belong to no world, no plane. I have no substance. Barriers can't stop me."

"There are barriers to everything. Perhaps you simply haven't found yours yet."

"You have a sharp mind," Saira said, impressed. "There is always the future. She keeps her secrets well, for now."

"For now?"

"Some things take time, or the right key. The impossible is always worth the adventure."

"And the past?"

"I go and come as I wish. I need only one small *thread* from someone's life to guide me to the beginning of their existence. I know every sentient being that has ever crossed their path and those before them. It's like putting together the pieces to a puzzle. Every life that touched them is a small part that makes up the whole of their essence."

"Thread? What *thread* brought you to me?"

"Yours." Saira laughed. "You're the attraction. I am curious why I never sensed you before. You feel familiar to me, yet you're newly arrived here. You are young looking but very ancient. A mystery."

"Am I supposed to make solving your puzzle easy?"

Saira shrugged. "No. Easy is always better, but not necessary. I'm a good listener for those who wish to tell me their stories. To the unwilling, the information is available for the taking. Most never feel my presence. A few, like you, sense my arrival. That's a mystery I've yet to solve. Perhaps you can tell me how you knew I was here."

"Not really. I simply felt that I was being watched. It's one of those things you know instinctively."

"As I said, a mystery yet to be solved. But, not now. This journey is about you. Will you tell me your story, or must I take another *thread* to your beginning?"

"I don't think you'd find that very pleasant, or even possible. Still, having company will be a good distraction. Have a seat. You do sit, don't you?"

Chuckling, Saira settled into a recliner. "It's the polite thing to do, isn't it?"

"I suppose. I'm new to all of this. Can I offer you something to drink, or are you not able to experience the physical since you don't exist?" The sarcasm was unmistakable.

"I'm not completely void of evolution's flaws," Saira replied, jokingly. "I appreciate many things in the physical realms. Unfortunately, eating and drinking aren't among them. The effects are rather disconcerting to some. Substances tend to flow through me."

"I see. In that case, forget I offered. As for my story, I hope you have a lot of time. It's long and complicated."

"Time means nothing to me."

"Right. I forgot. So...where to begin..." The demoness crossed her legs in human fashion, folded her hands on her lap, and leaned back in the recliner. "The best place would be the beginning. I'm called the Child, *Demon Child* to some. My life isn't only about me, but also about humanity in a way."

Saira's eyes widened slightly. "You certainly know how to grab someone's attention."

"My heritage," the Child replied wryly. "Anyway, before I was even born, I knew I was unloved and unwanted. I sensed it as I lay curled in the warm belly of my mother. It was awkward, to say the least."

"I can imagine."

"I doubt it. You had to be there," the Child said, her voice dripping with suppressed anger. "Dis sired me. Shortly after my conception, I grew aware of the world outside of Mother's

18

womb. It was noisy, hot and exciting. I couldn't wait to experience all that it had to offer.

Mother and Father's voices were easy to recognize. Hers was husky and vibrant. His, deep and booming. It resonated through my entire being whenever he spoke. But Mother, when she laughed...when she laughed, I was happy. Probably because she didn't do it often. Those weren't very happy times for anyone living here."

"Why?"

"Many lives were lost in a great battle."

"I remember. So you were born shortly after the end of the Great Battle?"

"Yes, and there were some who blamed Mother for the devastation."

"As I recall, there was plenty of blame to go around."

"There always is, isn't there? Anyway, I was sure Mother would eventually love me. How could she not? I was her child, her daughter."

"But she didn't."

The Child snorted. "No. She wasn't what you call mother material. I felt a great anger when I was born."

She shifted as if suddenly uncomfortable but then settled back in her chair. Saira could feel the deeply controlled anger still seething inside of the Child. Although seemingly calm, she was a tortured soul hunting for a way to ease the pain of being deprived of her mother's love.

"I can't imagine what being born feels like, let alone knowing from that very moment you're unloved," Saira said gently.

"Birth is painful. Not physically, but emotionally. Thrust from my wet, warm environment into the harsh glow of the Underworld was bad enough. I was snatched up, bundled into a soft, dry blanket and handed off into large, powerful hands. Father's. He took me away. I never felt Mother's touch, or heard her voice. The most important day of my life, and I was robbed of the most basic needs of a child. I never knew, really knew her until millennia later."

"And your mother is..."

"Lilith, of course. I assumed you knew. You do know who she is?"

"So that's why you seemed so familiar. You carry her essence. Long ago, I followed her *thread* here. She's a creation of a First Born."

"First Born? You mean the Twin?"

"That's what you call him. He and Dis are First Born. Only a handful of them are still around. Lilith was pregnant back then. I never thought anything about it. A pregnant demon wasn't that unusual. Besides, another *thread* pulled at me."

"You should have stuck around. It got rather interesting after that."

Saira's thoughts returned to the era of Lilith's creation. The Twin wasn't the only one experimenting with life. Worlds were evolving. Other First Born were playing with new life. Shaking off the memories, she apologized for her lapse in manners. "I'm sorry, please continue."

"Well, my parents would visit me whenever it suited them. Occasionally, Mother came to my room alone to ask my nursemaids how I was doing or if I needed anything. I don't know how much time passed before she actually walked over to my bedside to look at me. I remember staring into brilliant blue-black eyes and feeling lost. Then one day she smiled. It was faint but I felt so warm and..."

The Child glanced away for a second, her eyes growing moist. "And loved," she said, almost in a whisper. "I knew it was wishful thinking. Oh, Mother was clearly fascinated with me, but nothing more. She was incapable of real love. Satisfying her intellectual hunger and sexual appetite was more important."

"Love is a difficult emotion, especially for demons."

"Tell me about it. Father was no better, but I hated him less. Perhaps because I didn't expect very much from him. He never showed any real interest in me. I was a curiosity. After a few visits and instructions to my nannies, I rarely saw him. But Mother...my mother...I so wanted her to love me. To feel her arms wrapped gently around me, cradling me against her breast. I needed to hear the steady beat of her heart, feel the warmth of her breath as she leaned close to place light kisses on my brow or cheeks. Those were fantasies. My nannies were kind in their own way, but they weren't my mother. They weren't Lilith."

Saira knew exactly what the Child meant. There was only one Lilith. Loneliness was an emotion Saira understood well. She experienced moments when she longed for the closeness of friendship. Unfortunately, her travels never allowed her to stay in one place for very long. Contact with others was fleeting at best when life was an eternity. Saira remained silent.

"I remember my first steps," the Child continued. "From that moment on my keepers were incapable of controlling me. I escaped my *prison* at every opportunity to wander the Underworld. All the demons and minions knew who I was. They either avoided me or fawned over me. The latter actually encouraged me to be myself, and to take the revenge I craved for the disservice done to my mother by Adam and the Twin. I thought *they* loved me. It was nothing more than ambition."

"I see. By the way, do you have a name?" Saira asked, wanting to distract the Child from the emotions rising to the surface. She already knew the answer but chose not to disclose the extent of her knowledge, or her ability to read thoughts.

"Caelene. I am Caelene."

"It's a nice name."

"Yes. At least Mother gave me that much."

Caelene went on to describe how she had tricked Eve into eating the fruit from the tree of knowledge and then convinced her to get Adam to eat one. When Dis and Lilith learned of the deception, they banished her to the Netherworld for thousands of years. No one tampered with the Twin's experiments without

21

Dis' approval. Although at odds with him, the Underlord still retained a respect for the genius of his reclusive sibling.

Saira nodded in sympathy. She had never been to the Netherworld, and had believed it was an empty void. Clearly, she was mistaken. If Caelene had survived there, perhaps others were suffering the same fate. It could be an interesting journey.

"The story of Creation is an old one," Saira said. "Humans have rewritten the tale of Adam and Eve until it's more of a myth than anything."

"A myth lacking all the facts is all. I remember Mother's reaction when I first stepped from the mirror. She stared at me in awe. I think that was the first time she actually saw me for who I am."

Saira politely listened while monitoring the Child's actual memories. Like a movie on fast forward, the images racing through Caelene's mind filled in the unspoken words.

* * *

You are beautiful, Lilith thought when her daughter stepped into the room. When the Child didn't respond, she realized they could no longer communicate mentally. Everything had changed. Reaching out, she took her daughter's hand and turned her toward the mirror, placing her hands on the Child's shoulders. The two made eye contact with their reflections.

"Look," Lilith whispered.

The demonesses gazed into the looking glass. Lilith towered over the Child by several inches. Where her mother was tall with long, dark hair, the Child was short with waist-length, wavy red hair. Lilith's skin glowed a pale golden white while the Child's was a faint rose color. Brilliant green eyes met her mother's blue onyx ones in the reflection.

"Your hair. It's so long." Running her fingers across the top, Lilith noticed the small protrusions just above and to the right and left of her forehead.

Few in the Underworld had horns. Only those carrying the bloodline of the most ancient of demons had them, and even then, the horns disappeared over time. The same would probably have happened to the Child's if she hadn't been imprisoned in the Netherworld. Then again, her sire was the purest demon. She might still have had them forever.

Caelene continued her story unaware that Saira was watching the images in her mind.

"I was stunned when I saw Mother up close. I had never realized how beautiful she is. With long, dark shiny hair and those gorgeous eyes, she truly is the sultry seductress the other demons envy or desire. Even I can feel her sensual aura. It's not an emotion a child is comfortable with when it comes to a parent. Lilith could have any demon she desires...or all of them if she was ambitious."

"I believe that," said Saira.

"Then Father walked into the room. I was nervous, not sure what he would do or say. Mother freed me from my prison without his knowledge, although he had granted her permission to try. I doubt he believed she would succeed. Anyway, he's very tall and muscular with dark red skin. The ultimate male, strong, virile, and arrogant. For the most part, his only virtues are his deep affection for Mother and his sense of humor. He definitely has a soft spot for her. He finds it difficult to refuse her anything, and Mother knows that."

"That must be frustrating for him." Saira said.

"No doubt. He stared at me for a few moments. I knew he was assessing my worth. Mother put a stop to that by threatening to show up at all of his orgies. Father threw up his hands and left."

Saira laughed. Taking on Lilith was never a good idea, even for the Underlord. "A wise decision, I imagine."

"I agree. Lilith is very formidable when she wants to be, and at that moment, she was the loving, protective, powerful mother I ached for."

"Does she know about your future plans?"

Caelene lowered her eyes to stare at her interlocked fingers.

"Obviously, you're more than just a time traveler. You didn't say you were also a mind reader. But no, at least, I don't think so. But she probably has her suspicions."

"Probably." Saira was about to continue when she felt a tug pulling at her. Something was happening elsewhere that needed her immediate attention. Reluctant to leave such an interesting woman, she sighed. "Someone calls to me. Regretfully, I must leave now."

"Is that how it works? These *callings*?"

"Unfortunately. They come when they come. If they're strong enough, my natural curiosity compels me to investigate. Can we continue with this later?"

"I also have things to do. Do you know when you'll return?"

"For you, it will seem as if I never left. I will return at this exact moment. Don't let my plans interfere with yours."

Before the Child could reply, Saira was gone, leaving her alone with her thoughts, her memories and her plans. Caelene was glad her uninvited guest couldn't travel into the future. Putting those thoughts aside, she decided to check on Cerberus. Dis' pet and guard dog wasn't prone to excitement but something had upset him. As a child, she had loved playing with him. He still remembered her.

CHAPTER 6

DAKOTA WAS WORRIED. When they arrived home after the performance, Yemaya took a quick shower and went straight to bed without saying anything. Sliding under the sheets next to her, Dakota found her lover had already fallen asleep. She closed her eyes, hoping her spirit grandmother would sense her anxiety and visit her. Within minutes Dakota drifted into a restless slumber.

"I be right here, chile." The familiar voice of Granny was comforting. "What be troublin' yah?"

Opening her eyes, Dakota saw both her great-great-grandmother and Mari, Yemaya's ancestor, sitting beside her. Relieved, she gave both of them warm hugs.

"Oh Granny, I don't know. I think something went wrong during Yemaya's performance tonight. She's acting strangely."

"How so?" Mari asked.

"She seems preoccupied. I asked her about it, and she said she was just tired, but I know better. I can sense it. And tonight she went to bed without even saying goodnight. That's not like her."

"Maybe she be jest that. Yah knows the two of you don't get the rest yah needs, between all that travelin' and her performin' and such. I ain't even goin' into yer beddin' activ'ties."

25

"That's not it. And I sure wouldn't be criticizing us about our sex lives, considering you two never stop...from what I hear."

Rolling her eyes, Mari intervened. "Dakota, I think you're overreacting to what Maopa said. You know she wasn't criticizing you."

Dakota's green eyes suddenly filled with tears. "I know. Sorry, Granny."

"No need to be apologizin', chile. I knows yer worried. Maybe Mari can call her here ta see what's up."

Moments later, a very tired-looking Yemaya appeared next to them. She looked slightly confused and didn't say anything for a few seconds.

"Grandma Dakota, Mari, is something wrong?" she asked, regaining some of her composure.

"That's what we be wond'rin', deary. Dakota here be worried yer ailin'."

Yemaya shifted her gaze to her lover but failed to make eye contact, an action the two spirits noticed. Before the Illusionist could answer, Mari placed her right hand on Yemaya's left cheek, catching her by surprise.

"What bothers you, Daughter?"

"I have no idea, just a feeling. I think I may have been overdoing things. Maybe I need a break."

"No doubt. What kind of feeling?"

Yemaya shook her head. "I wish I knew. Tonight's show went well. At least what I remember of it. There are some moments of my performance I have no memory of."

"Tell us what happened."

Yemaya described each step of the routine. When she got to the part where the lid was lowered onto the sarcophagus, she hesitated.

"I remember lying in the darkness. Then I felt a shortness of breath. After that it is all a blank. The next thing I knew, I

26

was standing offstage in my apparition costume staring at my crew. How I got there I have no idea."

"Maybe you suffered from oxygen deprivation. That would explain the difficulty in breathing and consequent blackout," Mari said.

"True, but not how I escaped. Or managed to change costumes without someone's help."

"I wish I could give you answers," Mari said. "There has to be an explanation, though. Maybe you do need a break, a real vacation."

"That be true, chile."

* * *

"Listen, sweetie," Dakota said, turning to Yemaya. "Your tour's over. Let's pack our bags, get in my car, and go wherever the wind takes us. I can call Sonny and tell him we'll be incommunicado for a few weeks. Your brother and Reymone will handle everything back home until we return."

"I wish it were that easy." Yemaya rubbed her eyes wearily. "Somehow, whenever we go on a trip trouble manages to find us."

"That's because you don't go to the right places," Mari said with a grin.

"And that would be where?" Dakota asked.

"Here."

"Here? In the dreamworld?" Yemaya laughed. "You surely do not expect us to stay asleep for the next few weeks while we romp around in this place."

"Of course not. Don't be such a pessimist. While you and Dakota are here, Maopa and I will take care of your physical bodies."

Yemaya and Dakota looked at each other in confusion.

"And how are you going to do that?" Dakota asked.

"It's really quite simple. While you two play here, we play in your world. It'll be fun. I've never been human for long. Maopa can show me what it's like."

"And exactly what will you two be doing with our bodies?" Yemaya crossed her arms and raised her eyebrows in a questioning manner.

"Nothing you wouldn't do," Mari said, her pale blue eyes glinting with mischief.

"That is what I thought. I am not sure I like this idea."

Dakota, however, felt differently. "I do. Two or three weeks here in our favorite spot? No worries about our lives or bodies in the real world? What's not to like?"

"Dakota. Think about it. As much as we love and trust these two, do you really want them in control of our bodies and minds? Do you think people are not going to notice a difference?"

"Just your bodies, dear," Mari said. "Your minds will be here. What do you care what we do with the rest of you as long as you're enjoying yourselves? As for what others think, since when did you care about that? Besides, think of it as your gift to us for the wonderful time you'll be having here. And I get an opportunity to really experience being mortal."

Yemaya was clearly outnumbered. "Alright, as long as you make sure you do not get us arrested or in any trouble."

"Now, that ain't very nice," Maopa teased. "I'm thinkin' about a big, juicy steak with mashed taters and gravy, and showin' Mari 'bout bein' human."

"How do we do this?" Yemaya asked.

"Consider it done," Mari replied.

In a blink, the Earth Mother and her spirit partner disappeared. Yemaya glanced at Dakota and laughed.

"Mari should have stayed around a bit longer. This is not the best time of the month to be babysitting my body."

It took a few seconds for Dakota to understand her meaning. "Oh boy!" She rolled her eyes dramatically.

CHAPTER 7

THE SENSATION OF waking up was unique to Mari, as well as the feel of a bed, sheets, and Maopa's warm body wrapped tightly around her. Lying still, she listened to the sounds and inhaled the smells around her, trying to analyze each of them. For the most part, they were pleasant enough, with the exception of a faint obnoxious odor drifting from the air vents. The noises were a little more overwhelming, but she adjusted to them quickly.

Maopa's physical nearness was extremely enjoyable. It created a pleasant tingle throughout her entire body. Leaning slightly toward the still sleeping woman, she inhaled and smiled.

I think I'm going to like this experience, she thought, wanting to snuggle closer. Shifting slightly, Mari felt an uncomfortable bulge between her thighs. Reaching down, she tentatively touched the thick, bulky object.

"What in the world..." Frowning, she groped around the area. Mari rolled onto her back and threw off the sheets. She stared at the dark silk panties and again poked at the bulge. Pulling at the elastic waist, she peered inside at a thick white padding with a large red stain. Unsure of what she was supposed to do, she nudged the sleeping figure next to her. "Maopa."

Maopa groaned loudly, opened one eye, and peered blearily at Mari.

"What?" she grumbled. "Dang, girl, first time in a hunnert years I felt tired. I fergot what it were like." She made a face. "An' my mouth tastes awful."

"Maopa," Mari said again, slightly frustrated. "Look." She pointed at the offending object.

"Yeah? What about it? Yah be havin' yer monthly, that's all. Go ta sleep."

"Monthly?"

"Yah know. Means yah be at prime breedin' age. Tain't nothin' ta worry about."

"Oh! This is the *curse* humans talk about, right?"

"That be it. Yah be fecund when yer still getting' yer monthly. Only lasts a few days, mind yah. Now, how's about we get a little more shuteye. I'll enlighten yah on this partic'lar affliction when we wakes up."

Mari pointed at the sanitary napkin again and then tapped it tentatively with her index finger. "I can't sleep with this thing like that. It's uncomfortable. What do I do with it?"

Maopa sighed. She sat up, reached down, and snapped the elastic around her spirit partner's right leg.

"Nothin'. Them thar undies are holdin' it quite nicely. When it's done filled up with blood, yah throws it away and puts in a new one. Yah oughta be grateful they makes 'em more comf'table now. In mah day, twer whatever we could stuff down our drawers. Old rags was best, if'n we had 'em ta waste."

Mari felt her eyes almost roll back in her head at the thought of stuffing rags in her panties. She didn't even want to imagine what else might be used.

"Where do I throw this away and find another one? I thought humans were more evolved than this," she said irritably.

Now it was time for Maopa to roll her eyes. "Oh Lordy. I think yer gonna be in fer some surprises in the next few weeks, sugah."

Obviously, they'd never get any sleep until the situation was resolved to Mari's satisfaction. Maopa knew that wasn't going to happen for several days.

"I sure hopes this monthly is endin' and not beginnin'." Maopa grumbled. "Come on. Some of this be new ta me too. We might as well be gettin' yah took care of. If'n my grandchile starts her monthly, we're gonna be two mis'rible women."

Maopa grabbed Mari's hand and pulled her from the bed and into the bathroom. "Thank goodness we knowed about plumbin' and such. Bein' one of them voheeyurs helps a whole bunch even if'n it do seem a little preverted. " I'll scrounge around fer more of them paddin's whilst ya takes a shower."

Maopa wasn't sure, but she could have sworn Mari mumbled a few curse words as she walked awkwardly toward the bathroom.

Mari pulled off her panties and pad, tossed them in the small trashcan by the toilet, and then turned on the shower. After she climbed in, she slumped against the far wall.

Maopa rummaged through a few dresser drawers and quickly located an opened pack of feminine pads. She smiled. Mari was definitely going to remember this experience.

"Make shore yah dries off good!" she yelled over the sound of running water. "I'll be huntin' fer some of them fancy undies yer chile seems ta preefer. And don'tcha go throwin' away any of them clothes now...just that thar pad. I doubt yer daughter has enough undies ta last till we goes home."

Mari scrubbed her entire body with a large sponge that had been hanging on the showerhead. The warm water soothed the muscles that hurt for some odd reason, especially those on her lower right side. Soon, her body relaxed.

"If this is what being human feels like, I'm glad I'm a spirit. I won't last three weeks," she said loudly.

31

"Trust me, sugah, this be nothin' compared ta what yer gonna be feelin'!" Maopa yelled back, remembering the years she suffered through her cycles.

Grumbling to herself, Mari stepped from the tub and grabbed the soft white towel hanging on the rack. She quickly dried herself and tossed it on the floor just as Maopa walked back in.

"Yah cain't toss thangs on the floor like that."

"Where do I put it?"

After pointing to a large white basket in the corner, Maopa picked up the wet towel and dropped it inside.

"These be fer dirty clothes. A maid gets 'em later and washes 'em fer us. At least that's what I heered humans do nowadays. Used ta be slaves or servents did that sorta thang. Be thankful yah doesn't has ta do the scrubbin'."

Mari was about to comment when she belatedly realized she and Maopa were communicating verbally. Frowning, she tried to talk to her through mental images and failed.

"What be botherin' yah now?"

"We're talking."

"Well tarnation, woman. How else would we be a *conversin'*?"

"No. I mean we're *talking*. I can't hear your thoughts."

"What did yah expect? We be human now."

"Great. Some vacation this is turning into."

Mari wasn't sure why she was feeling so awful. Her stomach hurt, her back ached, and a slight pounding pain in her head was making her extremely irritable. Rubbing her stomach absentmindedly, she stared longingly at the bed in the next room.

"Maybe we can just stay in bed and call someone to bring us food," she said.

"Now, now. Don't be frettin' none. I promise yah, you'll be feelin' a whole lot better in a few days. Monthlies always makes yah irr'table. They calls it 'PMSing' nowadays. We called it the curse in my day. I heered they gots stuff ta ease the pain a bit. A pint of likker cured my aches and pains, but I don' figger they's much of that here."

After glancing around, Maopa found several small bottles of pills on the counter near the sink. She picked up each one and squinted at the instructions.

"Lordy, yah oughta see how tiny this here printin' be and the stuff they puts in these here jars. Words got more letters than a dikshuneerie. Can't be good fer yah."

Deciding on one that specifically mentioned pain and headaches on the label, she pulled on the lid. When it failed to open, she eyeballed it closely and noticed two small arrows.

"I'll be danged. They done made it so's yah has ta match them two errers ta open this thang. Most peculiar."

"I imagine some humans are a little slow and need help to figure it out."

"Ta take a lid off? If'n they screwed the top on no one'd need larnin' or help. Here yah go, sugah. Says ta take two with water and it keels the pain."

Mari tossed the small red capsules into her mouth and washed them down with water.

Maopa led Mari back to the bed and pushed her down on the mattress. "Lie back, and I'll get yah somethin' ta wear. Them pills oughta be makin' yah feel better in a bit." Chuckling to herself, Maopa searched through the drawers and closet for anything big enough to fit Mari. Finding nothing, she scowled.

"Gall darn it." She glanced around the room. Two large leather boxes sat on a chair in the corner. In one were several jeans and folded shirts. "Yer daughter shore do like ta keep thangs neat," she said pulling out a pair of worn jeans and a tee-shirt. Patting Mari on the shoulder, she continued her search for underwear. Eventually she found some in a dresser drawer and held them up. "Dang. Not much to them. And I ain't never seed so many delleekits in my life, all neat and orderly like. They kent all be Yemaya's. I useta have ta go without, most times. Tweren't nothing to it and it felt kinda liberatin'."

"It would be hard to hold this pad in place without them," Mari said.

"Yeah. Guess that's why they has so many."

Choosing a bright red pair, she held it up to the light and pulled on the sides a few times. "I figger they be fittin yah fine the way they stretches. Put these on and them thar garments. I be takin' a quick shower mahself."

Minutes later, Maopa returned, dressed in jeans and a tank top. Mari was still stretched out partially naked on the bed, one hand on her stomach. Her other arm was flung over her eyes to block the light.

"Yah okay, darlin'?" Maopa whispered, leaning down to caress her spirit lover's cheek with her fingertips.

Mari sat up and blinked a few times, surprised that she actually did feel better. Smiling, she clasped Maopa's hand and drew it to her lips. "Yes, those pills work wonders. Is this normal?" Standing, she pulled on the jeans and tee-shirt. Then, wrapping her arms around Maopa, she pulled her close. "You smell nice," she said, enjoying the warmth and softness of the woman in her embrace. "I'm beginning to see the allure of being human."

"It does has its good points," Maopa said, her voice muffled against the firm breasts. Feeling the strong arms wrapped around her, Maopa realized how much she missed the physical touch of another person.

"Adjusting to the spirit world must have been hard for you," Mari said, sensing her lover's thoughts. "I see why humans enjoy embracing each other."

"Tain't nothin' like it. Although they be some thangs a lot more enjoyable."

"I look forward to you showing me." The grin Mari gave Maopa sent a warm tingle straight to her groin, causing her to groan. "You okay?" Mari bent her knees slightly to make eye contact. "I hope this curse isn't contagious."

"Oh, it be catchin', alrighty, but no, I ain't havin' my monthly yet. If'n I'm right, though, it'll be comin' on soon."

"I should have taken more interest in women's evolution." Mari mentally kicked herself for neglecting her responsibilities. "I'd have made men suffer these things."

"Too late fer that, but it probably woulda made them a li'l wiser...and a whole lot more whiny."

"It's never too late for some things. One way or another, I'm going to make sure men get to experience—" Mari was interrupted by a ringing sound.

"Now what?"

"That be the teleephone. I seed my grandchile using these thangs." Maopa walked over to the device and picked it up. "Howdy. This be Mao...ummm...Miz Devereaux's place."

"Dakota? Is that you?" a male voice asked.

"Shore nuff."

"You don't sound like yourself. This is Sonny."

"Must be this here cold," Maopa said, faking a cough.

"Sorry to hear that. You really need to do something about it. You sound awful. Take some Nyquil; that'll make you feel better."

"Nyqueel?"

"Damn Dakota. You're either on some good meds or you're sicker than you realize. Is Ycmaya in? I'll give her a list of everything you'll need to take care of that cold. Can't let one of my favorite gals suffer, now can I?"

"No, sir...I mean...oh, don't yah mind me. Yemaya's right here."

Covering the mouthpiece, Maopa pushed it toward Mari. "It be Yemaya's agent, Sonny."

"What am I—" Taking the phone, Mari stared at it as if it were alive and then put it cautiously to her ear. "Sonny?"

"Hey, Yemaya. You really need to do something about Daks. She sounds awful."

"I'm taking good care of her, Sonny. What can I do for you?"

"As always, straight to the point. I heard your show was a great success. Congratulations."

"Thanks."

"Never one for words, are you? Anyway, I wanted to see if you've given any more thought to the European tour. I know you keep talking about retirement, but you're on a roll, and several people are clamoring for a commitment. A few have already offered to finance a world tour."

"How about I get back with you in a couple of weeks? I've just finished this show and don't feel like making a decision right away. Dakota and I are taking time off to discuss our future."

"Wonderful! It's about time. This can wait awhile. Besides, it's good business keeping potential investors waiting. Makes them nervous, and more willing to put up more money with fewer conditions," Sonny said. "Speaking of which, we really do need to go over your finances. Oops, sorry, but there's a call coming through from Hong Kong. I'll call you in a day or two. Tell Dakota to take care of that cold. Bye."

Before Mari could reply, Sonny hung up. "You know, I'm not sure this was such a good idea after all. I haven't a clue what Yemaya has in mind for her future," she said handing the phone back to Maopa.

"We jest have ta duck and weave 'til Yemaya and Dakota gets back. That's an old trick I learnt long ago."

"Good idea. Still, I don't want to play hermit. I'd like to take advantage of this opportunity of being mortal."

"We kin shorely do that." Maopa figured it would be a hoot seeing how Mari handled being human.

"Do you think we could go to a movie?" Mari asked. "I always wanted to do that. You know, enjoy the whole experience. Coke, candy, popcorn."

"Why, tarnation, I was thinkin' the same thang. I ain't never seed one. We kin sample all that junk food."

* * *

Giggling with an almost girlish anticipation, Mari and Maopa decided to check out the neighborhood first. Several hours and five hotdogs apiece later, they returned to the apartment, tired but happy. Mari had quickly adapted to monitoring her sanitary napkins.

"That Willie fella shore was gen'rous with his wieners once he knowed who yah was."

"He's a nice man, giving us hot dogs when we didn't have any money. We'd better find out where Yemaya and Dakota keep some if we're going to do anything else."

"Fer shore. As I recollects, most folk keeps it in small leather thangs. Wallets, they calls 'em. I seed one on Dakota's table next to the bed this mornin'." Maopa walked into the bedroom and returned waving a small leather object.

"Great. What movie should we see?"

"Willie says they puts a list of 'em in the paper under entertainin'. He shore gave me a funny look when I asked 'bout it. Let's look and see." Locating the movie listings, Maopa ran her finger past several titles until she came across one with three Xs. "This'un must be reeel good. They's three Xs by it. I'm guessin' that means extra special-like."

"That makes sense. We can call one of those cabs to take us. Any money in that wallet? I doubt if the cab or movie people will be as nice as Willie."

"Well, he shore is gonna have somethin' to tell his missus, ain't he? Givin' the Illusionist freebies cuz she ain't got no money."

"I hope Yemaya doesn't hear about it. I doubt she'd appreciate finding out she's on a handout list."

Maopa opened Dakota's wallet. Both peered at the money inside. Letting out simultaneous whoops, they smiled happily at each other. Minutes later, they were out the door and flagging down a taxi.

"Where to, ladies?" the driver asked. Maopa pointed at the address in the paper.

"We wants ta go thar."

The slight widening of his eyes would have been a giveaway to most people. Coughing slightly, he blushed. "You ladies must be new to Baltimore. You sure that's where you want to go?"

"Shore nuff. This'n is an XXX movie, ain't it?"

"It's definitely that, alright."

"Then we wants to go see it."

"It's your money, ladies."

Twenty minutes later, he dropped them in front of an old dilapidated building. Three large posters showing two semi-nude women in intimate poses hung on the dirty windows. Below the title was the phrase, "Woman on Woman Action! Two Babes Battle Interstellar Aliens Trying to Take Over Planet Earth!"

"A sci-fi!" Mari exclaimed enthusiastically. "I've always wanted to see one of those."

"Me, too."

Two hours later, they emerged and strode toward the main boulevard.

"Well, if'n that be a good movie, I ain't in no hurry to see a bad one."

"Neither am I. Those aliens looked ridiculous, and the acting wasn't even believable."

"Fer shore. That were the most piteeful thang I ever seed. Who'd go believin' them Marshuns had three peckers, let alone wantun people to b'lieve women folk would be havin' anythang to do with somethin' so ridiculous. Pfffft. I has to admit,

38

though, that popcorn stuff was mighty tasty. And that babe-on-babe ackshun...Well, them gals shore knows how to make whoopee. Why, some of them p'sitions looked downright painful. Ain't no way I coulda done that, 'specially with the rumatiz."

"How about before the rumatiz?" Mari asked in a teasing voice. Wiggling her eyebrows, Maopa grinned but said nothing. "I thought as much." Mari chuckled. "Still, they were interesting, don't you think?"

"Yep. Can't wait to try 'em out some more. How's about we go find another one of them XXX's tomorrow and see if'n thar's somethin' else they kin larn us."

"Works for me. Right now, I'm ready for another shower and a long sleep. I never knew what feeling dirty and tired meant until now. I'm not so sure I like it."

"Tain't nothin' to like or dislike, sugah. It just be the way it be."

Later, after eating a few more hotdogs with all the toppings, they returned to the apartment, showered, crawled into bed, and fell asleep instantly. Their 'babe on babe ackshun' would have to wait until another day.

CHAPTER 8

SAIRA APPEARED next to the bed and stared at the sleeping women. At first, she thought she was back with the Illusionist, but something was different. The energy belonged to someone else. Searching the human's thoughts, she found that Yemaya's essence no longer inhabited her body. Instead, a spirit named Mari had taken control of it. Recognizing her as First Born, Saira was pleased. This one had been more elusive than the others, Mostly because she was so reclusive. Switching her attention to Mari's partner, Saira was satisfied the other person was also human, or at least part of her was. She too was inhabited by a spirit, but one less mysterious than the Earth Mother. Still, the essences of both spirits were irreversibly intertwined, making them unique.

"All things are unique," a soft, low voice whispered, interrupting Saira's musings. Refocusing on the Illusionist, Saira found herself gazing into icy blue eyes. The woman had pushed herself up on one elbow, perhaps to better see who had invaded her bedroom and interrupted her slumber.

"True, but not all things are unique in their uniqueness," Saira replied, not surprised that Mari knew she was there. For some unknown reason, all First Born were able to feel her presence. "And most don't ever know I exist."

"I can believe that most are unaware of you. Who are you? Why are you here? Are you seeking Yemaya or me?"

"I'm Saira, a traveler. I seek both of you. She for her darkness, and you for your light."

"My daughter is not dark!"

"I'm not judging her. I'm merely satisfying my curiosity about her. She's an anomaly among humans. I need to know why. Part of the answer lies with you. As her ancestor, you're her light. Her strength to combat this darkness comes from you."

"Some of it, probably. But not all. Her partner Dakota is her real strength. She is a grandchild of Maopa. Yemaya and Dakota make a formidable pair."

"As do you and your companion. You are also contradictions. Maopa was once human. You, never. She's young and you're ancient. Even your love is contrary to the natural order of things."

"Love's always contrary. There's no logical explanation for it. It's the most unnatural of natural emotions."

"You're right, of course. My words were not chosen well, but were well-meaning."

Mari gave a slight nod. "So, what now? Have you satisfied your curiosity about her and me?"

"Almost."

"What is left?"

"Her darkness. It's different. There's a tremendous anger in it...an anger that wants to consume all that she is. One day it may destroy her."

"Never." Mari's reply was so quietly spoken, Saira almost missed it. "I will never allow it to happen."

"Even you aren't that powerful, Mari. Nor can you always protect her. She would never want that from you, or even allow you to try."

"She would have no choice in the matter. I'll destroy anything and anyone that attempts to harm her or Dakota."

41

Saira knew Mari meant every word. Her love for Yemaya was limitless.

"Have some faith in your daughter, Mari. She seems quite capable of battling her own demons. She's very fortunate to have you, though."

"As am I to have her."

Saira could see the Earth Mother's blurred thoughts as images raced swiftly through her mind. Mari was searching for her own answers to her daughter's darkness.

"This *beast*. I've thought a lot about it. Sometimes I think it's my fault. I should have taken more interest in my children—"

"It has nothing to do with you. The darkness is her weakness and her strength. It makes her the person she is... Yemaya."

"But where does it come from?"

"The universe is filled with darkness. Hers, however, feels familiar. Almost..." Saira hesitated, reluctant to voice her thoughts. Better to keep quiet than to speak and be wrong.

"Almost?" Mari asked softly.

"Nothing. I don't wish to misspeak of things I don't know."

Mari knew that pressing the apparition would be useless. Besides, she had her suspicions. Many *darknesses* had escaped into the light when Intunecat created it. Others appeared with the formation of the universes and the worlds within them. Mari suddenly thought of her other child...one she hadn't seen in a very long time...one that lived between the light and darkness.

* * *

Gaia was evolving slowly but steadily. Already she was sentient. Well past the stage of self-awareness, she still had a long way to go before reaching maturity.

Saira watched Mari's thoughts flowing through her mind. She had known about Earth's unique nature since its creation, but could never find the right thread that would take her to the planet's soul...until now. Mari's link to Gaia insured Saira of success. She was tempted to grab it. Unfortunately, now wasn't the right time to take that journey.

"You're worried about your first born," Saira said.

"Yes. Gaia is an angry child. One I can no longer control. Once she realizes her full potential, she will wreak havoc on the humans, and everything else will suffer."

"Why is she so angry with humans?"

"She blames them for the Earth's destruction. For her pain. I fear for my other children's future."

"Ah. So she is behind all the recent catastrophes. You have good reason for your fear. Too bad I can't journey into the future to find an answer for you."

"Is that the only thing you do? Search for answers?"

"It's who I am. The purpose of my existence. I already know where all things lead. Just not where they began."

"By lead, you mean the present."

"The present is already the past. I can't be everywhere at once; so many things, small things, escape me. They may seem insignificant at the time, but have unintended consequences. I'm naturally curious. I may know those consequences, but not the cause. The past gives me answers. I admit I would like to know the future, but that would create its own chaos. Besides, even I like boundaries."

"Have you never done anything else?"

"There isn't anything else. Why would I seek to become something I'm not? By our very nature, we are what we are. To attempt to be something we're not is a waste of time and energy. You're the source of all natural life on this world. Would you want to be something different?"

"No, but I believe we're more than what destiny wants us to be."

"We're always more than what we're meant to be, but never more than what we are. You are the Earth Mother, First Born. You could have ruled over the lands and seas had you been ambitious. Instead, you chose to let this world evolve on its own. Are you happy with your choice?"

"No. I should have done more."

"Exactly. You chose this path. It felt right at the time, but left you incomplete. I choose to follow the roads before me. They lead me to new adventures, new questions, and the knowledge that I'll never discover all that there is to discover. It's comforting to know I will always have that."

"I think it would drive me crazy, always searching for answers to questions," Mari said. "Tell me, how is it that you know Yemaya? She's never mentioned you, and I can't believe she wouldn't have picked up on your presence. She's more sensitive to unusual energies than most humans."

"So I discovered the other night."

"The other night?"

"During her performance. I inadvertently interrupted her concentration. Unfortunately, it was almost fatal...an egregious lapse of judgment on my part."

Mari was stunned to hear her daughter had almost died, and that she had never sensed it. She was sure she'd know if Yemaya was in mortal danger.

"What happened?" she asked, her rising anger evident in her tone.

"She felt my presence. It distracted her. There wasn't time to regain her concentration to complete the escape from the coffin before she ran out of air."

"Why didn't I feel this?"

"I don't know. Your connection is strong. Anyway, I normally don't interfere in events that are happening because I have no effect on them. This was different. I caused her failure and I was obligated to correct my mistake."

"So you helped her escape."

"No, I can't undo what's been done. I moved her forward to where she would have been had I not interfered. The past was then erased."

"Why not just move her back to the moment before you arrived?"

"It's easier to move one person forward than an entire world backward. I must be careful not to do anything that alters the lives of the living."

"Didn't you just do that?"

"Yes and no. Yemaya would have completed the illusion had I not been there. By letting her die, I was changing everything in the future. I corrected an insignificant glitch."

"What did she have to say about this?"

"Nothing. She's not aware of what happened."

"Oh, she's aware that something happened. She just doesn't know what and is troubled by it." Saira's ghostly image flickered unsteadily. Pale, clear eyes reflected her troubled thoughts. For the first time, Mari noticed several white glowing tattoos on the apparitions forehead and right cheek.

"This isn't good," Saira said. "She shouldn't remember anything."

"Then you two have something in common. You're not the only one who has questions or wants answers. How did you move Yemaya forward?"

Saira's laughter was soft, reminding Mari of the delicate tinkling of a wind chime.

"I didn't actually move her forward. The future's like a blank tablet waiting to be written upon. I wouldn't know where to place her until it arrives. I suspended her life force and waited until that moment. She shouldn't have noticed the change."

"But she did. When you leave here tonight, will I forget you?"

"No, you are First Born. Time is your partner, not your enemy. As it moves, so do you, believing there will always be a tomorrow. I believe the same. Unfortunately for humans, time moves backward. They have no choice but to wait for its arrival and hope they can make the most of the few years they have."

"You mean forward, not backward," Mari said.

"No. Time is like a river. It flows gently toward us and then moves on. Mortals impatiently wait to see what the future brings and then look backward at what it brought. Spirits, well most spirits, rarely dwell on the past. The present is all that matters to them."

"And you?"

Saira was impressed by Mari's inquisitive mind.

"I move with it, against it, or across it. It's easier to move forward than backward. Of course by forward, I mean to the point that is, not what will be."

"At least that much I followed," Mari said, laughing softly.

"Good. Anyway, the *threads* of the living are vast and complicated. It's difficult to follow them to their end because of all of the lives that intersect or branch away from the original *thread*. Imagine a spider's web, a labyrinth of twists and turns with infinite possibilities of choices, and all leading to separate but specific destinations."

"Don't you ever get lost?"

"All *threads* eventually lead to their beginnings. Once there, I need only turn around and follow it home."

"What about the future?"

"There's nothing for me to catch in that direction."

"I see. Where are you going next? Is my past going to be your new journey?" Mari didn't like the thought of Saira delving into her past. She was a very private person.

"No, I must return to the Underworld. There is a child there that intrigues me. Afterward, who knows?"

"And Yemaya? Are you done with her?"

"Probably not. There is still the darkness that calls to me. I need to discover its source."

"Will you let me know when you find out?"

46

Saira hesitated. "I can't," she finally said, reaching a hand up to brush several strands of white, flowing hair behind her right ear. "Disclosing a person's past to another can alter the future. What is to be would never happen. A future that was never meant to be would exist, and all life would be forever changed. When the time is right, you and she will learn what you need to."

"I think you like to talk in riddles, but I know what you mean. I've avoided intervening in events for a long time. It was a mistake."

"Mari, I've followed hundreds of millions of *threads* in my life. Things happen the way they do for a reason. Don't be so harsh on yourself. Had you interfered in life differently, your beloved daughter wouldn't be the woman she is today. She's special because she fought her own battles."

"She would be special under any circumstances."

"Maybe," Saira agreed. "I must go. Enjoy your stay in this world."

Before Mari could thank her, Saira was gone, leaving behind a very tired Earth Mother.

"If I keep feeling this tired, I won't be able to take much more of this mortal stuff," Mari grumbled before falling into a deep slumber.

CHAPTER 9

THE NEXT DAY, Maopa and Mari spent their time touring parts of Baltimore and watching two more XXX movies. Noticing that most people used credit cards to purchase items at the neighborhood stores, they quickly realized that plastic was the best way to pay for everything. Even the theaters were willing to accept them. Only Willie, the local street vendor, refused their cards, but was more than willing to give the two women all the hotdogs they could eat, free of charge.

On the third day of their adventures, Sonny called at a particularly rough time for Mari. Feeling bloated from her menstruation, and experiencing a bad bout of cramps, she was in a foul mood. Maopa decided it was better for Mari to stay in bed and let nature take its course.

"How yah feelin', sugah?" Maopa carried a bowl of warm soup into the bedroom and set it on the side table.

"Like shit," Mari growled.

"Well, yah shore have learnt to speak like most humans."

"If I have to put up with this, I'm entitled."

Maopa smiled. "Yep. The curse shore can do yah in."

"That's putting it mildly. If I ever volunteer to babysit a body again, I'm going to make sure I don't have to go through this. All I do is stuff pills down one end and those tube things up the other, and that damn pad is so bulky I'm totally uncomfortable when I walk. I'm not even going to go into bowel movements and such. How dignified is that for the Earth Mother?"

Maopa laughed. "I wouldn't rightly know, but yah has a point. Bein' human shore don't get yah no special priv'liges."

Mari sighed and wondered how much longer she had to endure this torture. She took the soup and sipped it gratefully, trying not to think about what the next two weeks was going to bring. Fortunately for her, the menstruation cycle ended that evening. She was so relieved at her newfound freedom, she let out a loud *whoop,* picked Maopa up and swung her around in circles, then collapsed on the bed, out of breath and exhausted.

"You're heavy," she gasped.

"Now, that ain't no way to talk to a gal if'n yer plannin' on frolickin' later."

"What was I thinking?" Mari said and laughed at Maopa's indignant expression. "Let's take a shower and see what mischief we can get into. That's always fun." Wiggling both eyebrows, she gave Maopa a rakish grin.

"Mischief be mah middle name, sugah."

"So," Mari said, "are you going to show me what's so special about girl-on-girl human sex?"

"Mah pleashuh." Maopa grabbed the bottom of Mari's tee-shirt and pulled it up and over the taller woman's head. After tossing it away, she put her arms around Mari and pulled her close.

Mari felt warm as Maopa's hands wandered up and down her back.

"What do I do?" she whispered, her voice husky from the sensations coursing through her body.

"Lets me do mah thang, then you'll know how ta do yourn'."

Maopa ran her fingers around the elastic waistband of Mari's underwear, slowly pulling her panties down, and then motioned for Mari to step out of them. Those, too, she tossed on the floor. Kneeling, she stroked the long muscular thighs with her fingertips and then leaned in to kiss the dark mound in front of her. Inhaling deeply, she nuzzled it gently with her lips and then proceeded to draw her tongue up Mari's stomach and along her ribs until finally capturing a breast gently between her teeth. Mari gasped.

When Maopa finally stood up, she made eye contact with the fiery blue eyes of her lover. Passion flared, and instinctively both spirits leaned forward, their lips touching tentatively for the first time.

Mari wrapped her long arms hungrily around the shorter woman, who unconsciously returned the passionate embrace. They fell onto the bed and began to enjoy their first moments of physical love. Then came another reality check.

* * *

As much as Mari was enjoying Maopa's attention, she wasn't sure about some of her own bodily reactions. The building up of tension, the spasms in her stomach, and the incredible tingling between her legs as her lover continually stroked her with her tongue was driving her wild...well, almost. The warm liquid running down her pubic area and thighs felt a little creepy. All she could think of, between the spasms of pleasure and a sudden urge to pee, was how messy human sex was, and she wondered if something was wrong. Finally, deciding she had reached her limit, she thumped Maopa's blonde head with the fingertips of her right hand.

"I'm sure this gets better with practice." *At least I hope so,* she thought, glad for once that Maopa couldn't read her thoughts. "But do you think there are any more clean sheets around?"

"Dang, woman," Maopa said, her head popping up. Clear juices ran down her chin. Mari jerked back slightly.

"Do all humans do this?" she asked, appalled at the wild-looking woman glaring up at her. Hair sticking up at weird angles didn't help the situation.

"Only them that don't have no spirits inside of 'em," Maopa muttered, shaking her head and wiping her chin with her right hand. "Here I be lovin' on yah and all you can think of is clean beddin'. I knows it be a long time since I done this, but didya hafta go and ruin the mood by thumpin' on mah head like that?"

"Sorry," Mari said, sheepishly. "You were really good. Really. It's just that all I can think of is how cold those wet sheets were when that damn sanitary napkin fell out of my underwear, and...well...you know the mess. You'd think I would have awakened instead of hemorrhaging all over the place."

"That weren't no him'ragin. Just normal woman stuff. Why d'yah thinks we calls it the curse?"

"I know. I know. Well, now I've gone and...and...Damn, I don't even know what I've done, but the sheets are soaking wet again. It just doesn't seem natural."

"Like ya'd even know what were natural. Of course it be natural. Them there juices is what lubreecates yah. Shows yah be enjoyin' yerself."

"Oh. Umm...I mean. I know I was enjoying myself...kind of. At least I think I was." Mari wasn't quite sure now. "Maybe I just need a little more practice."

"Not if'n this is how it's gonna be."

"Come on, sweetie. This was my first time."

Remembering her first experience and how horrified she'd been, Maopa relented. She gave Mari a quick kiss, hopped off the bed, and headed for the bathroom, hoping a quick shower would help her mood some.

"Don'tcha worry 'bout it. First times ain't never the best, yah know. We just needs ta go a little more slow is all."

Sighing with relief, Mari followed closely behind. "That's probably a good idea." Maopa grunted, but didn't say anything else. Mari's thoughts went back to the wet sheets. "Ummm...about the sheets."

Maopa stopped and turned to face Mari. "Yah shore do have a bug up your —"

"I'm not sleeping on these sheets," Mari said quickly, determined to get her way on this. "And tomorrow we're buying a new mattress. I can't believe how much body fluid humans lose. It's a wonder they made it this far on the evolutionary scale."

Maopa finally laughed, her irrepressible humor reappearing. She really didn't blame Mari for being disappointed, and somewhat disgusted. Sex was something you developed a taste for. The thought made her snicker quietly.

"I thinks yah might be overreactin' a bit, darlin', but don'cha think we oughta wait till we leaves? Yemaya has plenty of money ta spend, but buyin' new stuff every time we dirty it could get mighty costly."

Pushing the shower curtain aside, she adjusted the temperature to warm, trying her best not to laugh. To learn that the Earth Mother could be quite human amused her.

"Okay. We'll just turn it over again, but I'm not sleeping on it if it's still wet."

Maopa straightened up and bumped into Mari who had been standing directly behind her. Losing her balance, Maopa started to fall forward when she felt two powerful hands grab her by the shoulders and pull her backward.

"Dadburnit, woman. What in tarnation's wrong with yah?"

"Sorry, Maopa. I'm not adjusting very well to this physical stuff. Pretending to be Yemaya for a short time was so much easier than babysitting her body."

Maopa snorted. "Next time, maybe yah'll think before yah jumps in and volunteers us fer somethin'."

"Point taken." Mari released Maopa and returned to the bedroom. Staring at the bed, she felt as though the rumpled sheets were mocking her. She yanked them off and headed to the linen hamper. Several more sheets were stuffed inside, and another pile lay on the floor next to it.

Then she felt the moisture sliding slowly down her legs. After tossing the newest used set of sheets onto the floor, she stomped back into the bathroom, her legs slightly apart in an attempt to keep her thighs from rubbing together. Without saying a word, she pulled the shower curtain aside and climbed in next to a very surprised Maopa.

"Whoever makes those XXX movies should be shot," she said. "I'm beginning to think the X's mean exasperating."

Maopa snorted and then finished rinsing off, muttering under her breath.

Mari suspected her lover wasn't very happy at the moment. *I'm glad I don't know what she's thinking. Shit, I'm glad this will be over in a couple of weeks. Being human is tedious.*

Twenty minutes later, the two emerged from their shower feeling a lot better. Not having to wear a pad or poke a tampon inside of her was a huge relief for Mari. Remembering her first experience with a tampon, she shivered.

It had been awkward and painful. Even Maopa wasn't much help, although she tried to read the instruction page while Mari made an attempt to follow her directions. Aligning the small bullet-shaped object with the slightly swollen and tender opening of her vulva proved more difficult than she imagined. The first tampon went in crooked. Immediately, Mari knew something was wrong and fished around with her fingers before finally finding the string and pulling it out. Holding up the offending object, she shook it vigorously.

"You'd think you'd at least know what you're doing," she said accusingly and flung it in the trash. She grabbed a second one, ripped off the plastic wrap, and took special care to gently push it in. Feeling victorious, she grinned at Maopa, who was still squinting at the fine print on the instruction sheet.

"My grandchile needs ta get some bifocles. She don't see worth a toot. This here print gets littler and littler," Maopa said, unaware of Mari's success.

"We'll remind her." The Earth Mother already felt a lot better. She grabbed the paper and tossed it in the trashcan. "Let's go do something fun." And they had.

They decided to check out the Baltimore National Aquarium. Afterward, they hired a cab to take them to another small theater in a sleazy part of the city.

"You ladies sure you want to go to this place? You don't look the type to be watching this kind of stuff," the cabbie said.

"Just goes to show how looks are deceiving, doesn't it?" Mari said. "Besides, we're on vacation so we've decided to live large." She gave Maopa a questioning look. "That's the right phrase isn't it?"

"That be it, alrighty."

"Okay. It's your money."

Ten minutes after the movie began, Mari and Maopa walked out of the building shaking their heads.

"That were the most disgustin' thang I ever seed."

"Definitely. We can mark this place off our list. I can't even imagine why anyone would come here. Yemaya ought to report the owners to the authorities for allowing such disgusting behavior on the premises."

"I knows folks gotta take a piss now and then...but ta do it in front of ladies ain't fittin'. And yah was right ta tell him so."

"It's a good thing I'm not in my true form. That young man would learn a few things about talking to a spirit like that. I may just pay him a little visit later when I'm back to my normal self."

"Sounds good ta me. I'll help."

CHAPTER 1 0

INTUNECAT FELT the ripple as the intruder entered his realm. Only two entities had been able to penetrate the barrier between the light and darkness. This was not either of them.

He remembered the day Lilith had arrived unannounced and uninvited. The revelation that his once impregnable world was vulnerable was disconcerting, but he soon forgot about that while getting to know her. Afterward, he looked forward to her visits. Not only was she mentally stimulating, but he felt an inexplicable attraction to her. Her voice, her touch, her presence brought a warmth and light to his world that he would have thought impossible.

"Do you always go where you're not invited?" he asked, unable to see what he knew was there.

"Would you have invited me if I hadn't come unasked?" a voice answered.

"You're female." He sighed melodramatically. "Why is it I can't keep women from barging in on my space?"

"Do you wish me to answer your question?"

"Would the answer prevent you from coming in the future?"

"No. Only satisfying my curiosity will do that."

"Then by all means, show yourself. The sooner I give you what you want, the sooner you'll be gone."

A luminescent white cloud appeared in the darkness, its shape shimmering slightly before becoming a transparent haziness.

"Who are you?" Intunecat asked.

"I am Saira, a simple traveler."

"Simple? I doubt that. You've traveled to an unusual place. Do you always intrude where you're not welcome?"

"I go where I must. To be welcomed is not important."

"I see. How did you manage to find your way here?"

"I followed a *thread* from Mari. It guided me to you."

"Mari told you about me?" he asked, surprised the Earth Mother would reveal anything about him, let alone indicate a way into his solitary sanctuary.

"No. She keeps her secrets well. She hasn't betrayed you."

"But you said she guided you here."

"Not her. Her *thread*. You're a part of her past and her present, so your lives are forever joined."

"And this *thread* has to do with our joining?"

"Of course. Those you meet in your life and those they have met are forever connected to you, as you are to them. Existence creates many strands in lives and time, like a spider's web. In the beginning, only a few are woven but they quickly grow larger and more abundant, trapping everything that comes in contact with the web. It's very complex in its simplicity."

Motioning for Saira to sit, Intunecat offered her a drink. Although it wasn't something he required, he was fond of the ritual. Saira politely refused, but did sit.

"Why follow a strand to me? I assume you've been doing this for a very long time."

"Longer than even you can imagine. You're First Born, one of five. It's rare that I have the chance to meet one or a sibling."

"Sibling? I have no sibling," the Dark One said indignantly. "Those you speak of are not of my essence."

Intunecat believed himself to be the creator of light and therefore the oldest living being. He didn't accept that Dis or the Twin were in any way connected to him. And Mari, his interest in her wasn't in any way sexual. He had no need of such things. The mind was the attraction, and she had the sharpest mind of any entity he had ever met...well, with the exception of Lilith. Both were formidable creatures.

"So why come here now?" he asked.

"Now is as good a time as any. Opportunity and curiosity compelled me."

"Meaning you don't have a choice."

"I always have choices. I follow my compulsions but they don't control me."

"So you say."

"So I say."

Feeling slightly disgruntled at his inability to get the desired reaction from her, Intunecat changed tactics. "This conversation is going nowhere. What do you want from me?"

"It's what I wanted before I met you. I have my answer now."

"To what? You haven't asked me anything."

"I never intended to ask you anything. You wouldn't know the answer anyway."

Intunecat grumbled something unintelligible. He wasn't used to being thwarted, and frustration only added to his irritability. "How can you be so sure?"

"Because I am."

"Must you be so evasive? Do you do this to everyone you meet?"

"Do what?"

"Play games. Oh, forget it. Since you have your answer, perhaps you'll share it with me. Then at least I'll know why you came here."

"Like I said—"

"I know. To find an answer. To what?"

"I can't say. It isn't the time for you to know. Telling you could drastically alter the future. Even First Born aren't immune to the damage tampering with the unknown can bring."

"Alright, your work is done. Is there anything else I can do for you?"

"No, you've done more than you'll ever know. Thank you."

"Does this mean you won't be coming back?" Intunecat asked, his voice full of hope.

Saira grinned broadly. "Unfortunately, I can't answer that either. It will depend on those you meet in the future, or who meet you. Already you seek something from someone that raises new questions. One day, my curiosity will bring me here if the relationship prospers. The daughter of a First Born, who became the wife of a First Born eons ago, will make the future interesting if she should fulfill the desires of a First Born."

Frowning, Intunecat understood the human impulse to stomp a foot. He was about to ask her for an explanation when she vanished. Perhaps it was intentional or merely an oversight, but Saira had given him enough information to know what had drawn her to him.

"Females," he growled unhappily. "They can be so frustrating."

Immediately, his thoughts turned to Lilith.

CHAPTER 1 1

THE CHILD WAS relaxing in her chair, staring at the fire in the hearth. She had just spent the night conversing with several demons about her plans for the future—her future, and theirs, if they remained loyal to her. Now, she was wondering when the apparition would return, not realizing Saira was about to appear at the precise moment she had left. Soon, Caelene would remember the past differently, and Saira would leave, not realizing she had altered the future again.

Although aware of the Child's ambitions, Saira had no interest in them. Instead, she wanted to know more about the past, and so she continued their conversation as if she had never left, and listened to the demoness' thoughts closely.

Humans. Nothing but believers, dreamers and hypocrites, the Child thought. *If only they knew what I know. My plan has been more successful than even I could have imagined, but I'm jumping ahead of myself. I was telling of my involvement with them.* She continued telling her story.

"The Twin was furious at Adam and Eve's betrayal. He forbade them to eat the fruit from the Tree of Knowledge. They ignored his commandment, thus potentially dooming them to an eternity of misery in Paradise...only that wasn't to be. Realizing that his experiment had failed, The Twin blamed himself."

The Child shook her head. "And he should have. No serpent existed there before my arrival. Had he paid more attention to his creations, he'd have known that. When he finally discovered me, his own twin's child, he must have felt a profound sadness, and perhaps a sense of betrayal. Already, too many lives had been lost in the Great Battle over Mother. Now, Eve was displaying those same independent qualities. I remember watching Adam and Eve from the Netherworld. I truly did feel sorry for them when they knelt before their *God*, fearful of his wrath."

Saira listened to the story while she sought the *thread* that would take her into the past...a past that would reveal the secrets of the demoness and her role in the evolution of mankind.

* * *

"You have betrayed my trust," the Voice said with great sadness.

"Forgive us, Father," Adam replied, trembling in fear.

"Was it so wrong to want what you already have?" Eve asked, glancing upward at the dark cloud hanging over their heads.

The Twin pondered her question. It was a fair one, deserving of an answer.

"No, I knew the day would come when you questioned your existence. I hoped it wouldn't be this soon."

"Then why are you angry?" she asked.

Only Dis had the audacity to challenge him, with the exception of Lilith, of course. Now, Eve was doing it. The Twin's irritation subsided.

"I'm not angry with you, child. Only saddened. I can't allow you to remain in Paradise. You would never be happy here. You know too much now."

"Where will we go? What will we do?" Adam looked up for the first time. "This is our home."

"I've prepared a place. Your new lives will be hard, but you will have all you need to survive. Knowledge is power."

Before they could ask anything else, they found themselves standing on barren soil in a land devoid of animals or plants as far as the eye could see. The horizon looked foreboding, with dark shapes unfamiliar to them.

A small white bird suddenly appeared, circling above the stunned couple. When Eve glanced up, it swooped toward her and then flew away, only to return when they didn't follow. After several more unproductive attempts, it gave up and flew away.

"It wants us to follow," Eve said.

A slight nod was the only indication Adam gave that he had heard her. Neither knew how long they walked. At first, the journey was easy. Then they grew thirsty. Their bellies growled from hunger. Although these things were unpleasant, they could not compare to the excruciating pain from their blistered, swollen feet. Had they not stumbled onto a small oasis, they'd have perished.

The cool water soothed their tortured bodies. They stayed by the bubbling spring for three days, waiting for their injuries to heal. Fruits and plants calmed their stomachs.

"We can't stay here," Adam said, handing Eve the berries he had picked earlier. Eve nodded, returning half of the fruit to him.

"I know."

That evening, when the air was cooler, they left. Shortly afterward, the oasis vanished. Nothing remained but a withered palm and blowing sand.

* * *

"I needed to insure their survival if I was to succeed with my own plans," Caelene continued, unaware that Saira had seen everything. "I guided them to an imperfect world, but one they could survive in. Over time they flourished, and bore many children. The first were sons, Cain and Abel. Humans believe Cain slew his brother out of hatred for having been rejected by his God. Such absurdity. The Twin loved his creations. He simply became more reclusive and refused to intervene in their lives."

The Child stared pensively into the dancing flames of her fireplace. "He granted them free will to do as they wished. I think he hoped they would learn from their mistakes. I, however, was not so inclined to trust their judgment. The only reason they are here now is because I manipulated them in subtle ways to insure their survival and their evolution." Looking up, Caelene frowned. "Are you sure want to hear all of this?"

"Yes," Saira replied. Guilt was a burden Caelene had carried for a long time. By telling her story she might relieve some of it.

Caelene nodded before continuing. "Cain was a farmer who took great joy in tilling the soil and growing food for his parents and siblings. Abel, on the other hand, enjoyed caring for animals, providing the meat necessary to sustain his family," Caelene explained. "In order to keep harmony between the two, Adam and Eve divided the land, giving half to Cain for cultivation and half to Abel for his livestock. One day, several animals wandered into Cain's field and devoured much of what he had grown. In a fit of anger, he killed a bull and several cows. When Abel learned of his brother's actions, he confronted him, his own temper flaring.

A battle ensued, and Cain gave Abel a mighty shove. Abel tripped over the loosely tilled soil and fell, striking his head on a stone. He died instantly. When Cain realized what he had done, he fell to his knees sobbing. Hours later, Adam and Eve found their son bent over the still figure of his brother. Anger was not an emotion familiar to them. At least, that's what I think. Perhaps their love simply blinded them of his failings. Anyway, they forgave him." Caelene paused for a moment, remembering the look on Adam and Eve's faces—confusion and sadness. "Eventually, Adam and Eve realized their children needed companions. They couldn't mate with each other. The thought was so repugnant that they sent some of their eldest into the new world to seek others that may be like them. They discovered a primitive race very compatible for breeding."

"So you were responsible for both their downfall and their survival?" Saira asked. She had listened to the Child's words and seen her thoughts. Although she knew the answer, she wanted the demoness to say it aloud...to hear her own words.

"I did what I could. They needed help. The Twin abandoned them; who else was there?"

"Very altruistic."

The Child laughed. "I never said that, and I doubt you believe it. Of course, I had my motives. It was a way to get even with the Twin. What better blow to his ego? His experiment was a complete failure – he was a failure."

"And you think he's done nothing to help them since?"

"Oh, he tinkers with them now and then. They're in his blood."

"And what about you?"

"Me?"

"They're in yours too. You're Lilith's child, and she is the Twin's."

"We're nothing alike," Caelene replied angrily. "I am my father's daughter, not the Twin's. And Mother is no longer human. Besides, I'm more interested in my world. Humans can deal with their own problems now."

"As it should be. Thank you for telling me your story. Unfortunately, another calls to me again. I'm sure we will talk soon."

Saira disappeared, leaving a brooding Caelene alone with her thoughts. Her uninvited visitor had been an interesting distraction.

The Child needed to move forward with her plans. She rose and left her abode to rendezvous with several lesser demons and minions. If she succeeded, the Underworld would be hers.

CHAPTER 1 2

THEIR NIGHT STARTED with a mad dash to catch another late XXX movie, 'Invasion of the Alien Chicks', and ended with several hotdogs from Willie's Wiener Stand. Afterward, the two spirits retired to their bedroom and tried to duplicate the alien chicks' odd renditions of lovemaking.

Most positions proved to be too awkward or painful to be enjoyable. They suspected the women actors were faking their reactions. After several failed attempts at the popular sixty-nine, they collapsed in a fit of laughter and decided to call it quits.

"I tell yah, this jest don't seem doable ta me. I mean, ain't no way I can conseentrate on doin' yah when yer doin' me at the same time. I kept fergettin' what I was doin'."

"So I noticed," Mari said with a laugh. "I guess this is what humans refer to as multi-tasking."

"We ain't doin' that fer shore, and I can't believe them gals was doin' any better. They must've been pretendin'."

"I think you're right. No wonder Yemaya and Dakota are so tired. Trying to do this every night is exhausting."

"Shore is. Either them two be a whole lot fitter than us or they knows somethin' we don't."

Mari pulled Maopa close against her body and snuggled under the sheets. "At least this is pleasant. I think I'm finally beginning to understand why humans enjoy sex so much."

"About darn time too. I was startin' ta thank yah didn't have it in ya."

"Oh, it was in me alright. Although I have to admit I like your tongue much better than your fingers. Those nails are too sharp."

Maopa looked down at her fingertips. "Dang. I bit them off as fer as I could. They cain't get no shorter."

"Well, either Dakota doesn't use them like the women in the movies or she wears gloves," Mari said.

Both women thought about it for a few moments.

"Naahh!" they said simultaneously and giggled as they snuggled under the sheets.

Closing their eyes, they fell instantly asleep.

* * *

Mari's sleep was interrupted by a loud clanging. Outside the apartment window a low rumbling caused the curtains to flutter. Exhausted from her escapades with Maopa, she wasn't in the mood to have her much-needed rest interfered with.

When the noise didn't stop, Mari threw off the top sheet, walked over to the window, and peered between the blinds. The bright early morning light caught her by surprise. She blinked painfully.

Good deeds never...only a few more days, she thought rubbing her eyes. Below her window, two men were working. Each one picked up several large plastic bags from the sidewalk and threw them in the back of a huge truck. Then one pulled a large lever. The contents disappeared behind a moving door. A scrunching sound was quickly followed by the door reopening. The exposed compartment was empty. Mari raised the blinds and slid the window up. Leaning out, she called to the workers.

"Hello!" Apparently, they couldn't hear her because of the noisy machinery. "Damn," she muttered. "Hellooo! You two!"

One man glanced up.

"You want something lady?" he yelled back, his right hand cupped around his mouth.

"Yes!"

When he motioned to his ear indicating that he couldn't hear, she sighed. The worker reached over and flipped a switch. Immediately the noise lowered to a mild rumble.

"What are you doing?" Mari asked.

"Picking up the trash, lady. What did you think we was doing?"

"Oh. Do you take away everything people throw out?"

Looking at his partner, the man made a circular motion next to his head with his hand. The other man grinned and nodded.

"Well, yeah. That's what we do. We pick up the trash."

"That's wonderful. Can you wait a minute? I have some trash for you."

"We're on a schedule, lady. Once we finish loading the rest of these bags, we move on."

"That's okay. I've got it right here," Mari said.

She ran to the large pile of sheets and dirty clothes. Quickly sorting the blouses and jeans from the rest of the items, she scooped up the sheets and underwear, then hurried back to the window. Realizing there was too much stuff to push through at one time, she dropped everything on the floor, except a handful of items. Mari tossed them out the window.

"Sorry" she called out when she saw one of the workers covered by several pairs of women's panties, a bra, and sheets.

Scrambling frantically to remove the stuff, his eyes crossed as he looked at the black lacy bra caught on the bill of his ball cap.

"Hey! Are you fucking nuts?" he called out yanking it off and throwing it on the ground.

67

Leaning out of the window, Mari gave him a sultry smile and winked.

"That was rather rude of me. Please forgive me," she called back in her most seductive voice.

"Oh, uhh...sure. That's okay." Before he could say anything else, more sheets and clothes tumbled down next to his feet, barely missing him. "We ain't a laundry service, ma'am," he yelled.

"That's okay. If you'll just put them in that thing, it'll be fine," Mari said. "We need to get new ones. Those are dirty."

The trash collector motioned for the other worker to pick everything else up to put in the dump truck. The black lacy bra and a pair of deep purple panties, he stuffed down the front of his shirt.

"Wonder what that's about," she murmured to herself. "Thanks a lot," she called to them. "I wasn't sure what I was going to do with them, but you've solved a huge problem for us."

"Oh, that's okay, ma'am. It's our pleasure. Right, Randy?" he said to the other man.

"Sure is. Our pleasure. Really. No problem, miss." Randy pulled off his hat to scratch his head.

"Great. How often do you come here?"

"Twice a week. Mondays and Thursdays."

"Good, we'll probably have more by then. Should I just throw them down there for you to pick up?"

"Uhhh...I don't think that would be a good idea, miss. Someone might take them. The city don't like people going through the trash, you know. They leave a big mess behind. You just wait till you hear us and do what you did...that is, if you're awake."

"Okay, I'll listen for you. That thing would awaken the dead," Mari said pointing to the truck.

"Sorry about that. We'll try to be a little quieter from now on. Look, we have to finish up here. We're running a little behind schedule now. You got anything else you want to get rid of?"

Mari thought for a minute and then realized she had a small trashcan with some used sanitary napkins and tampons. Her first impulse was to toss them down also but decided it would be too much trouble for the young men to pick them up off the street and sidewalk. Maybe she'd put them in a bag later and toss them out the next time he came by.

"No. That's it for now. Thanks again." Mari closed the window and returned to bed, satisfied she had resolved a huge problem.

Seems like a waste to throw those things out. Hopefully, they recycle that stuff. I'll ask Yemaya about that.

Wrapping her arms around Maopa, she quickly fell asleep.

* * *

Waking up was always a long process, or so it seemed to Maopa. Eyes closed, she'd lie still, trying to make sense of her surroundings and the noises around her. It felt as though her brain was struggling to climb out of some deep, dark hole in its efforts to regain consciousness. In her earlier life, she had always been up before sunrise. Now, she could barely drag herself out of bed until well after the birds were up. The worst way to wake up was to the irritating ring of the telephone. Today was one of those days. Grumbling, she groped for the offending object.

"What in tarna...dang...Devereaux," she said, trying to collect her thoughts.

"Hello? Ms. Devereaux? This is Sandra at Dr. Winslow's office. I was calling to remind you of your appointment today."

"Appointment?"

"Yes. You're scheduled to get your physical at three."

"Oh. Well, cain't we do it in a few weeks?" Maopa asked, desperately trying to figure out what a fiseecal was.

"I'm sorry, Ms. Devereaux, but you know how busy the doctor is. We couldn't work you in for another four months. Dr. Winslow's going on her yearly 'Doctors Without Borders' commitment. She'll be gone for three months."

"Dang. Okay. Never you mind, dearie. We'll be thar at three."

"Thank you. See you here," the disgustingly cheerful woman on the other end replied.

After hanging up, Maopa rolled on her back and swore. Next to her, Mari was sound asleep.

How in tarnation can anyone sleep through all that noise? Maopa wondered before deciding they had better get going. Nudging the sleeping figure, she grinned when Mari growled slightly and slapped at her hand.

"Time we be a movin'. We gots ta go get a fiseecal."

"What's a fiseecal?" Mari opened one eye to glare at her partner.

"I don't know. Some dang thang Dakota does every year. It must be import'nt."

Maopa jumped up and started toward the bathroom when she noticed the dirty pile of sheets and clothes had been reduced to a small clump of jeans and blouses.

"What happened thar?"

"Some men took them away earlier this morning."

"Yah let men in here while I be sleepin'?"

"Of course not, silly. They were outside the window. I threw the sheets down to them. They put them in some sort of truck. Said it was their job. They come by here twice a week. That's convenient."

"I'll be danged. Seems like a waste, but if'n that's the way they does it, then it shore saves us from burnin' 'em."

"I imagine humans have outgrown burning their bedding, sweetie. It would be too wasteful."

"Yeah. They be into that recyclin' thang. Helps with savin' the planet. Well, we better be gettin' a move on it. I'm mighty hungry. Willie said he's got new wieners. He'll be wantin' us to try 'em out."

"Wonderful. I was getting a little tired of the others. Thought we'd try something else today, maybe after your fiseecal. I heard pizza was good. By the way, where are we supposed to go for this appointment?"

"Ain't got no idee, but Dakota's one of them thar note takers. I figger it'll be writ down somewhere."

After showering and searching the apartment, Maopa found a reminder note on the refrigerator with the doctor's name and address.

They showed it to the taxi driver, sat back in the seat, and waited patiently while he sped through the city streets, reaching the address in less than twenty minutes.

"Thank ya, Jose. The ride were quite entertainin'. Don't know how long we gon' be inside, though."

"No problemo, Mees Dakota. Thees streets I know like the back of my hand. I wait. Maybe I get a taco down the street."

Inside the office, they were greeted by the cheery receptionist.

"Good afternoon, Ms. Devereaux. Please take a seat. The nurse will be out shortly."

Maopa and Mari sat down near a stack of magazines and flipped through them.

"I never knowed people liked almost nekkid women so much. Would yah look at them pitchers. They shore don't have no meat on them bones."

"Maybe that's why the magazines are here...to show women what they'll look like if they don't take good care of themselves," Mari said, turning the pages.

"That's prob'ly—"

"Ms. Devereaux, the nurse will see you now," the receptionist called out.

Standing, Mari and Maopa started toward the door.

"Sorry, miss, but only Ms. Devereaux can go back. You can wait out here if you want."

"Over mah—"

Mari nudged Maopa with her elbow.

"I mean, um, Ms. Lysanne here..." She paused. "Look, either she comes with me or we leaves and yah keeps yoh fiseecal."

Looking confused, the receptionist relented. "That's okay. Go on back."

A woman in a blue shirt and matching slacks motioned them forward and pointed at an open door. "If you'll just step in there and put this on, we can get started." She handed Maopa a pale blue garment. Once the door was closed behind them, Maopa held it up and examined it for a few seconds. Made of paper, it was barely long enough to cover her breasts and lower stomach.

"This be a strange lookin' shirt. I ain't sure it'll fit over the rest of mah clothes. I figgers this here paper wudn't last five minutes if'n I moved around in it. What in tarnation does I need ta wear an ugly thang like this fer?"

"Maybe it's to keep something from spilling on you. You should probably do what she told you," Mari said.

Maopa slipped her arms in the sleeves, pulled the gown over her shoulders, and sat down. Distracted by the anatomical charts on the walls, she squinted at the fine print next to several lines pointing to different parts of the body.

"I ain't seen nothin' like this. Old sawbones in mah day had a few jars and sharp knives. That be it."

"Just goes to show how things change."

"Shore do."

A light knock on the door interrupted their chat. The nurse walked in and gave Maopa a strange look.

"Is something wrong, Ms. Devereaux?"

"Naw...'cept this is kinda small."

"Excuse me?"

"This...shirt. It be, I mean, it's a little small."

The nurse laughed. "I never realized you had such a good sense of humor. Dr. Winslow will be in shortly. I need to get your BP and temp. When the doctor's done, we can get your weight and draw some blood for the multi-phasic profile. You haven't eaten today, have you?"

"Only some of them wieners, but that was a few hours ago."

"That's not good. Next time we'll schedule you in the morning. You can come back tomorrow for the blood work."

Mari watched the nurse strap a large black thing around Maopa's arm and pump it up.

"We have this new digital BP reader," the nurse said. "It's pretty cool."

"Uh huh." Maopa wondered just how tight the woman was going to make the black band. "You ain't tryin' to squeeze my arm off, are yah?"

The nurse chuckled as she scanned the numbers and wrote them on the chart. Then she placed another object against Maopa's ear and held it for a second. Looking at that number, she wrote it beside the other number.

"Everything looks good so far," she said, handing Maopa another paper object. "Now, if you'll finish getting undressed, you can use this to cover the rest of you."

The nurse picked up the chart and left the two startled spirits alone.

"She don't mean..."

"I think she does."

"I'm supposed ta get bare ass nekkid and put this here on... and nothin' else?"

"That's what she said."

"Hell, I don' even know that woman."

"Apparently she knows you, or rather, Dakota. I wonder what your granddaughter was doing before she met Yemaya."

"Me too. I thank we gonna have a good talk, that youngin' and I."

73

"You'd better hurry up and put that thing on. I get the impression time means something to these people. Think of this as having a new adventure and doing Dakota a favor. Obviously these fiseecals are important."

Grumbling, Maopa undressed, put on the top, and wrapped the paper drape around her waist. Pulling the edges together, she held them tightly with her right hand. After another knock on the door, the nurse walked in, pushing a large metal box on wheels.

"Good. Hop on the table, and we'll get the EKG done. The doctor will see you after that. Lie back and don't move."

Before Maopa realized what was happening, several small patches were stuck to her ankles and chest. The nurse attached wires to them and pushed a button. The machine spewed out a small strip of paper with crooked lines. Then the nurse removed the wires, pulled off the sticky patches, and walked out of the room, pushing the box in front of her.

"Be right back," she said.

"Well, if'n that ain't the most peeculyar thang I ever seed," Maopa said, sitting up and swinging her legs over the side of the table. Kicking them back and forth like a small child, she looked extremely unhappy.

"It definitely was different," Mari said, not quite able to suppress a smile. "Wonder what's next?"

A soft knock on the door prevented Maopa from answering. In walked the nurse, followed by a slender black woman.

"Hi, Dakota. How have you been feeling since your last visit?" Reaching out to shake Maopa's hand, the doctor glanced at Mari curiously. "I'm sorry. I don't think we've met. I'm Dr. Winslow," she said, smiling slightly.

"I'm Yemaya, Dakota's friend."

"I see. You're the first friend she's ever brought in during a pap test. You must be more than just a friend," Doctor Winslow said, her brown eyes sparkling with humor.

"You could say that."

"Good. It's about time she found someone and settled down."

Maopa squirmed slightly as Dr. Winslow turned toward her.

"Something wrong?"

"This dang blasted paper is stickin' to my rear end."

Looking at the nurse, Dr. Winslow chuckled. "You didn't order that cheap stuff did you?"

"Certainly not."

"Well, check into another brand. I can't have my patients walking around with paper stuck to them."

Dr. Winslow pulled her stethoscope from her jacket pocket, snapped the earpieces in place, and picked up the heart monitor. Reaching out, she gently pried the material from Maopa's fingers and pushed it aside.

"Something you're not telling me?" she asked. "And why the hillbilly accent? Are you trying out for a role in that new play, Mountain Mary? I heard the director put out a call for women with a country accent."

Maopa glared at the doctor, but decided to ignore the question.

"Tain't nothin' wrong with how I be talkin'. Ah'm a little nervous, yah might say."

"I guess that's as good an explanation as any," the doctor replied. "After all these years, I still don't know why you act so nervous when you come here. I'd think you'd be used to this by now. We'll get the rest over with quickly."

Placing the heart monitor against Maopa's chest, she listened to the steady rhythm.

"It's a little fast. Inhale and exhale." She moved the stethoscope to Maopa's back, and then listened to her stomach.

"It all sounds good. Your stomach's a bit noisy. Any discomfort down there?"

"If'n yah askin' whether or not I has a bellyache, no I doesn't."

"Good. Swing your legs up, and we'll get the unpleasant part over with." Frowning, Maopa swung her feet up and sat rigidly, her legs straight out in front of her. "Lie back, Dakota. I swear if I didn't know better, I'd think this was your first time."

"Just shows what you thank. Yah knows it ain't so."

Dr. Winslow hesitated and glanced more closely at her patient. "Have you been checking your breasts every month?"

"They been gettin' a lot of checkin' lately." Maopa grinned and winked at Mari.

Dr. Winslow smirked. "I imagine the checker hasn't found anything unusual."

"Ain't heerd no complaints."

Dr. Winslow placed her fingertips on Maopa's left breast. As she began pushing and moving her hands around, Maopa watched, curious about the strange action. The right breast was treated the same. Then her stomach was pressed in several areas before the doctor seemed satisfied.

"Everything feels good. No lumps. Keep checking them though. I want you to have a mammogram before your next visit. Rachelle will schedule it for you."

"Shore nuff, doc." Maopa didn't have a clue as to what a mammogram was and wasn't sure she wanted to know.

Signaling for the nurse to adjust the stirrups, Dr. Winslow told Maopa to slide down and put her feet in them.

"Now, hold on thar. Them thar...them there...them thangs ain't...aren't...are steerups."

"Dakota, are you feeling okay?"

"Excuse me, Dr. Winslow," Mari said. "Dakota has been entertaining me a lot lately. We've probably been overdoing it a bit and didn't get home until early this morning. You know how lack of sleep can affect people."

"Lack of sleep?" Dr. Winslow asked with a smile. "I know it can do a lot of things, but this is the first time I've ever seen a complete personality change from it."

"Trust me. With the schedule we've been keeping, Dakota definitely isn't herself at the moment."

"Oh, I believe that. Okay, look. I promise I can be in and out in seconds. Would you just lie back and relax?"

Maopa slowly slid into position and grumbled again about more paper sticking to her butt. Relaxing slightly, she let the nurse guide her feet into the stirrups.

This be damn awkward, Maopa thought, trying to maneuver the paper down to cover her legs. Dr. Winslow pushed the cloth drape up slightly and gently nudged Maopa's knees apart while the nurse moved the lamp closer.

"Good. Slide down a few inches more."

Sighing, Maopa did as she was instructed, but found it difficult. The edge of the table cut into her butt cheeks, and her groin ached from forcing her knees apart.

"It shore be drafty down thar, doc."

"This will only take a minute."

A faint clicking sound made Maopa look toward the nurse. The woman had just picked up a small metal device and was squeezing a clear gel onto it. She turned a small wheel on its end. The object slowly closed. Then she handed the instrument to Dr. Winslow, who bent down and lowered her head beneath the drape.

"Okay. I need you to spread your knees a little wider."

"They don't get no wider than this. I ain't no plucked chicken, yah know. These here legs only opens so far."

"Look, Dakota. Would you just open wider so I can do the pap?"

"I'm telling yah, they don't get no wider. Jest get done down thar."

With an audible sigh, Dr. Winslow reached down to gently spread the labia with her fingers. "This is going to be a little cold."

Maopa stiffened when she felt the doctor touching her pussy but decided to keep quiet for the moment. When the device was pushed inside her vagina, though, she let out a whoop, reached down and smacked the doctor on the back of her head. Dr. Winslow's head popped up like a cork in water. Instinctively, she jerked the object out.

"What the hell?" Apparently without thinking, she started to rub her head and smacked it with the instrument. "Son of a bitch!" she yelled. The device flew from her hand, landing with a loud metallic clang on the floor at the nurse's feet. Surprised, the nurse jumped back and bumped into a silver stand. It fell against the counter, rolled a few inches and then crashed to the floor. Seconds later a woman flung open the door. Dashing in, she stepped on the device and fell face first into Dakota's spread legs. Embarrassed, the woman pushed herself away and bumped into Dr. Winslow, almost knocking her into Mari.

"Dadburnit, that's it! I ain't lettin' yah go and stick that thang up my peehole no matter how many times yah done it 'afor."

Maopa leaped off the table, grabbed her clothes, and marched out of the room, oblivious to the pieces of paper stuck to her butt. Three very stunned women were left behind wondering what the hell just happened.

Mari looked sympathetically at them.

"Must be the wieners. I told her not to put all that stuff on them. Maybe we should postpone this until another day, Doctor." She picked up Maopa's shoes and quickly followed her indignant partner.

Outside the building, Maopa stood in her blue top and partially torn drape. One hand was clenched tightly around the paper remnants while the other held the top garment closed. Her clothes were tucked under her right elbow. Mari waited patiently next to her. Several people walked by, gave them strange looks and continued on. Jose pulled up in his cab, but didn't say a word as he opened the passenger door.

"I ain't knowin' what this world has come ta, but ain't no way no one's gonna go stickin' thangs up my cooch like that," Maopa said, growling.

"Well, it really isn't yours," Mari replied.

"It be mine at the moment, and until my grandchile gets it back, I ain't lettin' no dang woman poke me, lessin' I sez she ken. Tarnations, I ain't even knowed that woman!"

"I certainly can understand that. I guess we know what a fiseecal is now. I wonder what she meant by pap test. It sounded important."

"Well, if'n yer askin' me, I says it meant pokin' at pussies. Why anyone would want ta be doin' that beats the tar out of me. It be downright humileeatin'.."

Deciding to get dressed, Maopa yanked off the gown and then glared at the driver's mirror. "And don't yah be lookin' back here like that, or I'll turn yah into a toad."

After pulling on her jeans and top, Maopa felt her stomach growling. "I'm hungry. How about we gets one of them pizzas and then goes ta check out that mall we seed a ways back?"

"Works for me." Mari gave her a hug. "This will be over soon enough. Let's hope we survive until then."

"I twern't aware of no partic'lar time for us ta be back," Maopa said.

"Well..." Mari replied hesitantly. "I think Dakota and Yemaya will be more than ready to return home soon. I certainly am looking forward to the peace and quiet of our world."

CHAPTER 13

THE BOOKSTORE WAS tucked away in a small wing of the mall. Mari knew about books, but had never actually handled one. Grabbing Maopa by the arm, she dragged her through the open doors. They stopped in front of a large display of picture calendars.

"This is amazing." Her eyes moved from one photo topic to another. Reaching out, she gently ran her fingertips across the smooth front-page photo of an artist's rendition of a dragon. Painted in vibrant colors, the creature seemed to be staring at her.

"And to think that once they were plentiful," she sighed softly.

"There actually be dragons?" Maopa asked.

"Yes. Not many, mind you. Most were hunted down and destroyed."

"I figgered they was just stories, made up for the youngins."

"They are magnificent creatures and highly intelligent. Unfortunately, their one weakness is the need to hibernate in the winter. In the past, humans hunted them in their lairs and killed them out of fear and ignorance. Dragons are like all living things. All they want is to grow up, find mates, raise their young and grow old. Most of all, they want to live their lives soaring high above the land and seas, enjoying a freedom no human could ever experience or imagine. It's almost impossible to do that nowadays. Unfortunately, the remote places are disappearing. I fear they will be extinct in a few centuries."

"That be true with many thangs. Couldn' yah make a speshul place for 'em?"

"It's not that easy, but worth considering," Mari said. Strolling through the aisles, she gazed in awe at the thousands of books lining the shelves. "So many words, so many thoughts," she murmured, almost to herself. "Can you imagine what it must be like to put your thoughts down in a physical form like this? How tedious it must be."

"It shore be a lot of work, I'll give yah that."

Stopping in front of the history section, she pulled out several books, glanced at the cover pages, and turned them over.

"History books. Moments in time. Can anyone describe what really happens when they see only one piece of such a huge puzzle?" Mari was just thinking out loud. Not looking for an answer to her question.

She put the books back in their proper places, and moved to another section. A smile appeared on the Earth Mother's face. "Look at these. Aren't they wonderful?" She picked up a large, thin book with a comical looking creature standing on a colorful pointed mountain. She flipped open the pages and began reading the lines.

"Dr. Seuss. I've heard of him. Listen to this. 'Oh the Places You'll Go...'"

Speaking softly, she read the entire story to Maopa. Her voice was low and gentle, filled with awe at the feeling the words instilled. When she finished, she slowly closed the book and ran her hand over the cover lovingly. A quiet applause surprised her. Glancing around, she saw several people smiling and then moving away, each seemingly touched by the moment.

"He shore do have a way with the words."

"Yes, he does. I think I'll buy this."

Maopa smiled. Another cover caught Mari's attention. It displayed a man, a woman, and several funny looking dinosaurs eating plants. As she read the story inside, she frowned and then laughed aloud.

"Humans have such vivid imaginations. They are so good at telling fairy tales. Listen."

She quickly read a few passages from the story. "Can you believe someone actually believes dinosaurs lived in harmony with Adam and Eve?"

Maopa snickered.

"And this author thinks they were all vegetarians," Mari said.

"I heerd about this awhile back. They calls it intelleegent somethin' or other. It be the latest explanashun of how thangs came ta be."

It was Mari's turn to snicker. "Like I said, humans have great imaginations. Let's pay for my book and check out Victoria's Secret. According to the magazine ads, they have some great women's underwear."

"Somethin' we be sorely lackin'," Maopa said. "If'n yah hadn' thrown them out the winder, we mighta been able to scrub 'em some."

"Maybe the bras, but not the panties. Those things are so delicate they tear at the slightest touch."

Maopa made a comical expression. "Yep. Found that out last night. They shore weren't made ta last, but they be a lotta fun."

Mari slapped her arm, grabbed her elbow, and pulled her toward the checkout counter. After paying for the book, she asked for directions to the lingerie shop. Package tucked under her left arm, the Earth Mother wrapped her right around Maopa's shoulder, happily anticipating their next adventure and ignoring the strange glances from several people they passed.

CHAPTER 14

THE NIGHTCLUB WAS full. A small crowd of women stood outside chatting, hoping to gain entry. Fire codes limited the number of people to one-hundred-fifty. Lilith knew that Agra, her business partner and head bartender, was right. They were going to have to put in an addition soon or find another location.

Scanning some of the ads in the local paper, she circled a couple of possible prospects. Tomorrow, she'd contact her real estate agent and ask her to check them out. She set the newspaper down, stood, and adjusted her blue satin dress. The material felt wonderful against the skin, but she hated the way it slipped up whenever she sat.

Leaving her office, Lilith nodded to several of the regulars and walked over to an empty chair at the far end of the bar. Most of the customers knew it was reserved for the owner, and those that didn't were quickly enlightened. Agra placed a glass of wine in front of her and leaned her elbows on the bar.

"Full house again, boss. When are you going to put in an addition?"

"Soon. I'm still waiting for the estimates. If they're too high, I may look for another location. Sometimes it's cheaper to buy than build."

"True. I was thinking about that. If we find another place, perhaps we could get something big enough to convert part of it into living quarters for some of our girls."

"I'm not building a whore house, Agra. It's hard enough keeping the cops out of here without attracting their attention that way."

"Actually, I was thinking more about a place they could have some personal space. Kind of like a sanctuary. Many of them still live in hellholes, although if literal, that would be an improvement. Others are getting too old to keep working. They won't be able to pay their rents once they stop. We can't abandon them."

"I'd never let that happen. I'll see what my agent comes up with. As long as the girls understand hanky-panky in the home won't be tolerated."

Before Agra could reply, they felt a disturbance in the energy around them. Simultaneously, the two demonesses glanced at the main entrance, wondering who had arrived that held such power. When Yemaya and Dakota walked in, Lilith frowned.

"Something's not right," she said. "Get them their usual drinks and table. I'll be over in a while."

Agra left the bar and strolled over to greet the two women. "Hey, Yemaya, Dakota. Glad to see you." Without hesitation, she walked over to a secluded table occupied by three women and whispered something to them. Glancing at Yemaya and Dakota, they grinned, saluted them with their drinks, stood, and walked to the bar for refills. Agra signaled for Mudada to clean the table. "Have a seat. I'll get you your usual."

"Thanks," Mari said, not sure what she was talking about but deciding whatever it was, if Yemaya drank it, it had to be good. Taking Maopa's arm, she guided her toward the table and pulled out her chair. The courtly gesture didn't escape Lilith's attention.

84

After placing a Corona in front of Dakota and glass of wine near Yemaya, Agra grinned. "Didn't think we'd be seeing you for a while. I heard there was a glitch in the show the other night. Someone said you decided to take a break."

"An exaggeration." Mari picked up the wine and took a sip. "This is really good. What's it called?"

A sudden elbow in the ribs caused her to spill some of the drink. She gave Maopa a surprised look.

"Oh, we took your suggestion and brought in the Chablis you recommended. Only the best for our favorite customers. I'll get some extra napkins for you in case Dakota decides to nudge you again." Agra winked at the small blonde.

Walking away, she knew something was different about them, but couldn't quite figure out what. When she passed Lilith, Agra stopped her for a moment and whispered in her ear. Lilith patted her on the shoulder and continued over to the table.

"Yemaya, Dakota, how are you doing?" she asked.

"Tarred," Maopa said, taking a sip of the beer and coughing.

"Tarred?"

"Tired," Mari said. "She's got a slight cold. I guess it's affected her speech." She laughed and nudged Maopa with her elbow.

"Ah. It can do that. I heard your last performance caused quite a stir. Some of the gossip columns are saying you're pushing the limits too much. That idiot, Jenny Collins, is even insinuating you might be suicidal."

"I don't pay attention to gossip," Mari replied. "Who's to say we aren't on vacation? What's more relaxing than unwinding with a few friends in one our favorite haunts?"

"Yep. We decided ta check out the place," Maopa said. "On a weekday night, that is. Say, this beer is purty good, but do yah have anythin' stronger?"

Lilith couldn't stop herself from raising both eyebrows in surprise.

"Beer or mixed drink?" Lilith asked.

"Oh, mixed I thank...umm...thank yah, I mean."

"I'll be right back."

After Lilith left, Maopa leaned close to Mari.

"Trying to talk like that grandchile of mine is damn hard."

"So I've noticed. Are you sure you should be drinking something stronger? I've heard alcohol can affect brain function."

"Good. I won' need ta explain mahself. We can blame it on the likker."

"True."

Standing at the bar, Lilith watched Yemaya and Dakota chatting and puzzled over the change in them. The unusually high energy emanating from them would have been enough to arouse suspicion, but there was more. The darkness within the Illusionist seemed smaller, weaker, as though it had skulked into some dark corner and was trying to make itself invisible. When she had first met Yemaya, she felt the *beast's* rage and frustration. It was biding its time, waiting for the right moment to seize control.

The demoness had no doubt Yemaya could control the *beast* as long as Dakota was alive. The possibility remained that it would consume the Illusionist in time. Tonight, her darkness was hiding, afraid of something or someone...and that someone wasn't Yemaya. Then there was their peculiar speech. Yemaya never spoke with contractions and Dakota didn't have a strong accent. Something was definitely wrong.

"Here you go," Lilith said, placing several napkins on the table and wiping up the spill with another. "Mudada's bringing you one of the house specials. I think you'll like it."

Within minutes, a short, fat woman waddled over and plopped two brightly colored drinks on the table. Giving the two customers a toothy, yellow grin, she grabbed her crotch and adjusted herself. Getting no reaction from either of Lilith's guests, she grumbled a few words and left.

"Sorry about that," Lilith said, and chuckled. "She doesn't have a lot of class, but she's good at what she does."

"Not ta worry. She 'minds me of someone I knowed a long time ago."

"Why, Dakota. You're going to have to tell me about her," Mari said in a teasing tone. "I never knew you liked that type of woman." The second elbow to the ribs caused Mari to flinch. "Would you stop that? I'm sore enough without you adding more bruises to this body."

Before Maopa could reply, Lilith decided to distract the two.

"Try the drinks. They're called Royal Fucks, and it's become one of our biggest sellers."

Mari and Maopa took sips.

"This is good."

"Shore is."

"I'm glad you like it. Don't drink too many. They have quite a kick. Now, if you'll excuse me, Bertha's having a problem with someone. I'll be back later."

"We look forward to it and thanks."

After Lilith left, Maopa and Mari glanced around the room, observing the various women and their interactions with each other. Two tables over, a deep masculine-sounding voice was describing how much its owner loved her Harley.

"I tell you, once you ride this baby, you ain't ever gonna want to get off her. She's sweet and purrs whenever I take her out. I clean her up every time I take her out. I tell you she's a better ride than any woman I've ever known. Just thinking about her almost makes me wet."

"If you say so." Her companion seemed totally uninterested in the subject.

"Do human women really discuss their girlfriends like that?" Mari asked. "If I was Harley, I'd be quite angry."

"They talks 'bout anythang and everythang. Worst gossips yah ever knowed."

"Well, I hope Harley finds out this woman talks about her like that and kicks her butt."

"At least she seems to appresheeate her."

"I suppose. You want another Royal Fuck? Looks like you drank that one pretty quickly."

"And look who be talkin'. Yah done drunk every drop of your'n."

Mari laughed, liking the slight euphoria she was starting to feel. "Another won't hurt."

Before they could even signal Agra, Mudada arrived with two more. She placed them on the table, grabbed the empty glasses, and left.

"I think we hurt her feelings."

"Yeah. She shore seems ta be sulkin'."

"Did you notice the group by the dance floor? What's with the black clothes and makeup. They look like cadavers."

"Maybe they's sickly."

"Could be. They sure don't look well."

* * *

Two hours and five Royal Fucks later, Mari wasn't feeling so well. Maopa wisely stopped at three after realizing that Dakota's body had little tolerance for alcohol. Besides, someone had to make sure they got home safely, especially after it was obvious the Earth Mother was drunker than a skunk.

"Yah doin' okay, sweetie?" she asked, noticing Mari's glassy eyes.

"Shoh nuff." Mari tried to focus on her lover's face. "If this room," she said with a burp, "would just stop moving." Glancing around, she saw Mudada cleaning glasses in the corner of the bar. "Hey, Muddy. Two more Roiel fugs."

"I thank yah need ta go easy now, Mari. Yah don't know what them thangs gonna do to yah in a couple hours."

"Oh pfffft! Whaz one more?" She burped again. "Damn. Whaz with the gas?"

"Not to worry, sugah. It's nat'ral."

Sitting at the end of the bar, Lilith watched with fascination as the Illusionist and the journalist consumed several drinks. At one point she was about to order Agra not to fix anymore, but realized Dakota had stopped drinking and was monitoring Yemaya's intake. Signaling to Agra to make the next two drinks "virgins," she waited for them and then carried them over to their table.

"Thought you might like these," she said, setting the drinks on the table.

"There you go...Moppy. Lilly..." Feeling dizzy, Mari rubbed her eyes and looked around. "Maybe I should go... relieve myself."

"I'll show you the way." Lilith took her by the arm. "Be right back," she said to Dakota.

Steering the inebriated woman through the maze of tables, Lilith guided her into the bathroom and located an empty stall. "Do you need help?"

"Nope. No prob...lem." Patting the demoness' arm, Mari gave her a lopsided grin. "Be right back."

She banged into the door and then backed up a step before advancing toward the toilet. After turning around cautiously, she yanked down her jeans and plopped down on the seat.

Lilith turned her back and blocked the entrance to prevent anyone from witnessing what must have been a very unusual event. She could imagine what Yemaya would feel like in the morning from the drinks, let alone having some fan or paparazzi snap a photo of her peeing.

At the sound of a flushing toilet and swearing, Lilith swung around in time to see Yemaya trying to zip up.

"Here. Let me."

Lilith gently pushed away the clumsy hands, grabbed the zipper, and slowly pulled it up. Then taking Yemaya's arm, she led her back to the table and handed her over to Dakota. After watching the two for several hours, Lilith had a pretty good idea what was behind the change in the two women. Why was a different matter.

"Listen, Dakota. I'm not sure what's going on here, but I know you two aren't who you seem to be. Yemaya would never allow herself to get drunk, nor would you."

Maopa knew Yemaya and Dakota liked Lilith, but wasn't sure how much they trusted her. Not wanting to break any confidences, she decided discretion was probably a better choice.

"Now ain't a good time to be discussin' this. Best I take Yem home. She's gonna be hurtin' real bad in a few hours."

"I suspect that's putting it mildly. Do you want me to call you a cab?"

"We'd shore appreeshiate it."

Maopa gave her the address of their apartment. Mari, who had lost interest in everything but sleeping, had settled down with her head on her folded arms.

"I don't...feel so...good," she mumbled. Popping her head up, she groaned as the room began to spin. "I'm hungry," she said, suddenly feeling ravenous.

"I don't thank that be a good idee, sweetie."

"Please. It might make me feel better." Rolling her eyes, she looked to Lilith for support.

"I can get Agra to cook up a couple of hotdogs from the grill, if you think that will help."

"Hotdogs? I love hotdogs."

"Hotdogs it is then."

Several minutes later, two hotdogs arrived, fully loaded. Maopa refused hers. Mari quickly downed the first and then looked longingly at the remaining hotdog lying on the table.

"Yah gonna hate yuhself fer it later, but go ahead," Maopa said. *I figures it'll be the last time yah gets this drunk, anyways,* she thought.

Feeling full, Mari was more than happy to head home. The alcohol was playing havoc with her head, and she could feel the *beast* moving restlessly around its cave, seeking escape from the effects of the alcohol. Obviously, it didn't care very much for Royal Fucks.

The ride home in the taxi made Mari feel the same way. Once in the apartment, Maopa let Mari go straight to bed instead of showering. Only time would solve this problem.

"Thank goodness I ken hold my likker. Then agin, I always could," Maopa muttered, slipping beneath the sheets and sliding next to her unconscious partner.

CHAPTER 15

MARI FELT BAD...really bad. She opened her eyes and flinched from the pain caused by the nightlight near the bed. "This isn't good."

The room did a quick spin. Mari swore she'd never drink another Royal Fuck no matter how delicious it tasted. Her stomach apparently agreed. It growled ominously. Within seconds, the discomfort turned into a totally new feeling. Fortunately, the bathroom was only a few feet away.

Maopa wasn't sure what woke her, but she was immediately aware that Mari was no longer in bed. The bathroom door was closed. A narrow beam of light glowed from beneath it.

"This ain't good. Ain't good a'tall."

Quietly opening the door, she peeked inside. Mari was kneeling on the floor, her head hanging over the edge of the tub. The smell of vomit permeated the air. Maopa grabbed a washrag and soaked it with warm water.

"Oh sweetie, I knowed this was gonna happen," she murmured, pushing the hair away from Mari's face. Wiping her forehead first, she switched to her cheeks and then mouth.

"I feel awful," Mari said. "What's happening?"

Before Maopa could reply, Mari grabbed her stomach and heaved several times. Fortunately or not, she had expelled everything from her stomach.

"Yah sufferin' a hangover. Nothin' a few hours of sleep won' cure."

"I was asleep. This woke me up. I think I've killed my daughter."

"Nah, she's tough. No li'l hangover's gonna kill her. Humans goes through this all the time. You'll be dandy in a few hours."

Another bout of the dry heaves left Mari exhausted, sore, and not too sure Maopa was right. This vacation was definitely not what she thought it would be.

* * *

After sending Yemaya and Dakota off in a cab, Lilith returned to her office to work on her bookkeeping. A knock on the door interrupted the silence.

"Come in."

"I think you need to get out here," Agra said. "You have another guest."

"Who now?"

"I'm not really sure, but some of the customers aren't very happy at the moment."

"Lead on."

The sound of wolf calls and grumbling met her at the entrance to the main room. Standing next to Bertha, who for the first time looked extremely uncomfortable, was a tall, handsome man in a dark suit and flowing cape.

"Hey, good lookin'," a woman yelled from one of the tables. "It's women only, but for you I'll make an exception. You bring yourself right over here next to Felicia and me, and we'll make you feel right at home."

"Shut up, Cracker. Maybe you'll fuck a man, but some of us don't care how good-lookin' they are. Men don't belong here."

"Yeah," another piped in.

"Meeeowwww," a voice said from across the room. "Looks like we're gonna have a cat fight, ladies."

Completely ignoring the comments, the stranger focused on Lilith and gave her an imperceptible nod.

"Ladies," she said, "I think I'll decide who can come in here and who can't. This gentleman happens to be an old friend of mine, so be nice."

"I thought you was a dyke like the rest of us," Cracker yelled.

"Speak for yourself, Cracker," a woman answered back. "No one said this was a fuckin' dyke club. It's a women's club. Besides, ain't you the one trying to put the make on this guy?"

"Enough!" Lilith glared at the two women and then glanced around the room. Immediately things settled down, although she heard a few grumbles about some people having more privileges than others. Lilith snapped her fingers loudly and signaled Mudada and Bertha to remove the complainers. "Let's get one thing straight, ladies. This is my nightclub. I make the rules. I expect you to obey them. If you don't like them, go elsewhere, but never, and I mean never, ever challenge me again. Now, for all of you who have so kindly decided to stay, the next drink is on the house."

A loud cheer drowned out the whining of the two dissidents as they were escorted to the door and ordered off the property. Two young women, who had been standing in line waiting to get in, pushed their way in after their I.D.s were checked by Bertha.

Lilith walked over to the man and smiled. "This is an unexpected surprise. What's so important you would leave your sanctuary to come here?"

"I've missed our talks."

"Uh huh. Let's go to my office so I can find out what's really behind your visit. As pleasant and enjoyable as our talks have been, I doubt you would come here just to chat."

*　*　*

Not wanting to disturb him, Lilith didn't speak while the dark figure paced back and forth. His unexpected visit to her nightclub had caught her by surprise.

"Lilith's Den" was a "women only" establishment. Her customers took the restriction very seriously. Seeing a man strolling in as if he owned the place, no matter how handsome he was, didn't make them happy. A knock on her office door interrupted her musings.

"Enter," she said.

Kali walked in carrying two glasses filled with ice and two cans of soda. "Here you go," she said, laying the tray on her boss' desk.

"Thanks, Kali. That's all for now. Call me if you need me."

Kali backed up a few steps, abruptly turned, and left.

"She doesn't like me," Intunecat said. He walked over and picked up his drink. "I don't know what it is about this stuff, but I find it interesting. Almost addictive, if such a thing were possible."

"Anything is possible."

"I'm beginning to believe that."

"Why are you here, Intunecat?" Lilith asked quietly. "The mortal world isn't exactly your favorite haunt."

Intunecat lowered his long body into the chair next to her desk. "I'm a spirit, not a ghost," he said with a chuckle.

"Oh, right. I forgot," she teased. "So, back to my question."

"Well, you visited me in my realm. I thought I'd just return the favor."

"Uh huh."

95

"I think you have the wrong impression about me. I've been here many times. Mortals fascinate me."

"That, I believe. Still, you'd never come here except on business. What's up?"

"Do you know an entity called Saira?"

"The Traveler? I've met her. A rather interesting creature. Why do you ask?"

"She visited me a few days ago...uninvited."

"I imagine it was rather disconcerting having her show up in your realm. She definitely comes and goes at will. I'm surprised she found her way to you, though."

"Apparently she found me through Mari, or should I say, those *threads* she follows. Seems no one can hide from her if she finds one of those things."

"I know. Too bad we can't see them. Imagine all the things we could achieve."

"Or the damage that could be done."

Lilith thought about his words and agreed. Anyone capable of returning to the past could easily alter the future. "It would be chaos, wouldn't it?"

Intunecat rubbed his chin. "Maybe that's why Saira is the only one of her kind. At least, I hope. Too many Travelers would disrupt the fabric of time. As it is, she's created enough disruptions already."

"True," Lilith said. "Do you think she's aware of what she's really doing?"

"No, and that's probably a good thing. If she realized she changes things every time she comes in contact with someone, it might destroy her."

Lilith turned the idea over in her mind. "I'm not so sure of that. Saira has been around even longer than we have. I can't believe she isn't aware of the impact she has on lives. No one is that innocent."

"Innocent? No. More naïve. She calls herself a traveler and describes time as if it were a giant web. For us, and the mortal world, time is only the present and the past. For her, it isn't so linear. It goes in all directions. Her only limitation is the future."

"True. Of course, all of us go about our lives not noticing the effect we have on others. Most of us don't even care. Why should she be any different? Saira is compelled to find answers to questions. She follows these *threads* to their source, believing her trips have no effect on the lives she touches, not realizing she is changing both. In a way, she is the spider checking every strand in her web, making sure everything's okay."

"That's a huge leap from time traveler to spider," Intunecat said and chuckled. "Still, your point is well taken. What if time really is a giant web, something that's continually growing larger and larger, and what if her sole purpose is to travel its strands, making sure there aren't any weak or broken strands?"

"Which would make her a guardian of both the past and the future." Lilith said. "It's an interesting concept."

"Well, if we're right, I hope nothing happens to her. She's the only thing standing between us and chaos. Should even one *thread* break, the entire web could collapse," Intunecat said.

"And time would break apart."

"Such a cataclysmic event would bring about the total destruction of everything."

"Of course, this is all conjecture, but it's not why you came to visit me, I'm sure."

"Actually, it was...and to ask you something."

Lilith raised both eyebrows. Intunecat looked uncomfortable, almost boyish.

"I was wondering. When you first came to visit me...you know, I like my privacy and my realm isn't easily found. No one should be able to enter it without my permission. Then you walked in. And now Saira. My world isn't as secure as I thought."

Lilith wanted to laugh but realized it might hurt Intunecat's feelings. Standing, she walked around the desk and knelt down next to him. She knew how hard it was for him to reveal this weakness.

"I'm so sorry, Intunecat. That was unforgivable of me."

"Oh, don't get me wrong. I'm glad you came. You've made my existence more interesting," he said, smiling slightly. "It's just..."

"Two intruders in such a short time is disturbing," Lilith said, saving him the embarrassment of finishing his sentence.

"Exactly."

"I wouldn't worry about it. I seriously doubt if anyone else is going to be able to enter without your permission. Saira obviously can go anywhere she wants."

"And you?"

"Me? I can go wherever there's darkness. I imagine it's because I was created from the darkness. It's a part of me."

"In your case, I'm glad. I enjoy your visits. It brings a certain light to my dark world."

"Thank you. I enjoy them too."

Intunecat put his glass down and stood up. "I think it's time to leave. I wouldn't want your bartenders barging in here thinking I was abusing you in some way. Angry feminists can be quite a handful."

CHAPTER 16

MARI GROANED, not sure whether she could endure much more of the lovemaking, two bodies, slick with sweat, sliding back and forth. Lips continually locking and unlocking. Tongues warring for dominance.

It just isn't fair, she thought and closed her eyes temporarily, trying to control the feelings coursing through her body.

When the hand slipped down between hot thighs and began stroking the warm, wet lips, Mari pressed her knees together for a moment and inhaled deeply. Fingers moved slowly up and down, spreading the runny juices across their tips, making them easier to insert into the silky smooth opening.

"Jesus Christ!" Maopa exclaimed, unable to control her own mounting passion.

Mari felt her heart pounding faster and faster as the tingling spread.

"Jesus has nothing to do with it," she murmured. "But I'm beginning to understand what humans see in this."

"Oh yeah," Maopa said, squirming.

Fascinated at the unexpected pleasure she was feeling, Mari closed her eyes for a few seconds, not sure how much longer she could endure the exquisite torment.

"You like this?"

"Oh, yeah. Baby, you're hotter than a witch's clit."

Short labored gasps, followed by low moans, filled the room but even the darkness couldn't hide the passionate embrace as the two women fought for control, each trying to be the dominant lover.

Hands moved rapidly over moist, slick hair, through warm silky lips and into the deep, dark recesses of their most intimate spots in an attempt to bring about the ultimate climax.

Fixated on the building emotions and their struggles to maintain some semblance of control, Mari and Maopa both jumped when the scream erupted during the climactic moment.

"Baby, that was the best."

"For me too. Maybe we can do it again sometime. I'll call you if I'm ever back this way."

"But I thought you loved me. You said..."

"What? I never mentioned love. Love is for fools. I take what I want and give pleasure in return. You, kiddo, weren't bad, but I've had better."

Picking up her leather jacket, the tall women leaned down, kissed the small blonde on the lips and walked from the room.

For a moment there was unbearable silence; then the lights came on. Mari and Maopa blinked. People were moving down the aisles, heading for the exits.

"Phew! That were the best XXX movie yet. I ain't never felt quite like this 'afore."

"I know what you mean. I'm ready to cool off. You want to go for a walk?"

"It might help some, but I ain't so shore it's gonna cool me down. I'm feelin' hornier than a horny toad."

"We passed a park on the way here. Let's go sit for a while. I don't have the energy to do much else."

Grabbing Maopa's hand, Mari pulled her lover up and slipped out of the theater. Glancing back at the title, Lady Cop in Toyland, Mari grinned. "This might be worth seeing again."

"Damn right. Them toys they was a playin' with looked mighty interestin'. What was they called? Dildies?"

"Dildos, I think. It was a little confusing. The lady cop kept talking about geckos and turbo rabbits."

"Yeah. I kept lookin' ta see what in tarnation a geeko was. Finally figured it were a fancy name for them vibrat'rs."

"It confused me too."

Holding hands, they walked until they found the small park and a secluded bench.

Mari felt the urge to kiss Maopa and leaned down, her warm breath caressing her companion's cheek and lips. Just as she was about to make contact, a flash distracted her. Looking up, she noticed a thin, slimy looking man standing near them with a camera. He tipped his hat and grinned.

"You two should really get a hotel room," he said and hurried off.

"Who in tarnation was that?"

"Probably a fan of Yemaya's. I guess we'd better head on back to the apartment. We certainly aren't going to get any privacy here."

"Not afore we buy some new bed fixin's. We done run out."

The last thing Mari wanted to do was shop. Trying to think of a reason not to, she glanced up and down the street and noticed a sign two blocks away that gave her hope.

"That man. He said something about getting a hotel."

"Yep. Guess he thanks we was gonna do it right here."

"Why don't we get a hotel, then? It would save us having to go shopping, and honestly, I don't feel like it."

"Me neether. That's a mighty fine idee."

Grinning like school girls, the two marched hand in hand toward their destination. Once inside, they strolled up to the check-in counter.

"Can I help you?" A young woman smiled amiably.

"Yeah, we wants a room."

"How many nights?"

Mari looked at Maopa, who raised her hand and counted on her fingers. "Seven nights."

"Let me check and see if we have one...We have several rooms and five suites. What kind of bed do you want?"

"What kind has yah got?"

"Kings, queens, and doubles."

Mari and Dakota gave each other a confused look.

"What's the largest one yah gots?"

"King, of course."

"Then we be wantin' a king."

"King it is. Will you be putting this on your credit card?"

"Shore nuff."

Mari nudged Maopa and pulled her aside. "You know we get the bed pretty wet. I don't want to be sleeping on cold, wet sheets and bedding. It kills the mood."

"Yeah, for me too."

Turning back to the clerk, Maopa grinned. "We wants a diff'rent room each night, if'n yah don't mind."

"Excuse me?"

"Yah heerd me. A diff'rent room. We don't like sleepin' on wet beddin'."

"Oh, that's no problem. Laundry always makes sure the sheets are dry before they put them on the beds."

"Oh, it ain't that, darlin'. We tend to get them mighty wet with our activ'ties, if'n yah knows what I mean."

Maopa winked and gave the woman a mischievous grin.

"Oh...ohhhhh! Um, sure. Sorry. Um...let me see."

Quickly typing on the keyboard, clerk leaned toward the monitor and stared at it. "Here we go. It's going to be a little complicated since checkout is at eleven, but it's doable. Tonight you can have 132 and tomorrow 221. You know, we do change the sheets every day, so switching rooms really isn't necessary," the receptionist explained.

"Does yah change them thar mattreeses too?"

"Well, no, that's not neces..."

"Then we wants a new room every night."

"Okay. It'll take a while to reserve the others so I'll do it later, if that's alright."

"That'll be fine, chile."

Maopa pulled a credit card from her pocket. She handed it to the clerk, who did a double-take.

"You're Yemaya Lysanne!" she squeaked, looking at the taller woman. "You're the Illusionist. Oh my God. I've always wanted to go to one of your shows."

Mari wasn't sure how to respond and looked at Maopa.

"We be tryin' to have some privacy, so if'n yah don't mind, we'd appresheeate it if'n yah'd keep quiet about this."

"Oh. Sure. I'll just tell the boss. She knows how to keep the public out."

"Thank yah much, and what yah be callin' yuhself?"

"Scamper."

"Scamper. That be a heck of a name."

"It's a nickname, but I like it better than Mary."

"Well, Scamper, would yah mind orderin' us a couple of pizzas while we makes ourselves at home?"

"Not at all. Anything special?"

Maopa gave her the list of ingredients and then the two went to their room, anxious to try out the new positions they had observed in the movie. Once inside, Mari remembered she had forgotten to ask the clerk something.

"I'll be right back," she said and dashed out the door.

Scamper was busy clicking away on the keyboard. Mari gave a slight cough.

"Oh, Ms. Lysanne," the clerk said looking up. "I didn't hear you."

"That's okay. My friend was wondering about something. Perhaps you could help her out."

"Sure."

"She's been hearing about some toy shops in the area. Are there any near here?"

"Toy shop? Well, there's a Toys For Them six blocks from here. They have a nice selection of kid's toys."

"That's not exactly the kind of toy she was interested in."

"Well, that's the only toy shop near..." Scamper gave Mari a strange look and then blushed. "You mean *toy* shop, don't you?"

Mari smiled and nodded.

"There's one just around the corner to the right for a block, then two blocks to the left."

"Thanks, Scamper."

"Oh, and Ms. Lysanne." The clerk leaned closer, lowering her voice. "Tell her to check out the Jack Rabbit series. She'll enjoy it, and so will you."

"Thank you." Amused, Mari headed back to the room, making a mental note to leave a message for Yemaya to send Scamper tickets to her next performance.

CHAPTER 17

THE WATER WAS COOL, but not cold enough to chill the heated bodies of the two women floating tiredly on the surface. Apparently, even the spirit world couldn't provide an infinite amount of energy to replace what they were burning during their stay in Mari's realm. Yemaya and Dakota didn't know how much time had passed since their ancestors' departure. Time wasn't relevant.

"I'm not saying I'm tired of this place," Dakota said, "but I don't think I've ever felt this exhausted."

Yemaya gave her a lazy smile. "I know what you mean. I have lost count of how many times we have made love. If we count the times we practiced a little foreplay..." She let the sentence drop knowing Dakota would understand.

"Oh yeah. There's more things to sex than sex sometimes. You'd think while we are here, our energy would be limitless."

"Maybe being human prevents that. This is not our world."

"I suppose. Speaking of which, I wonder what's happening back home."

"I try to avoid thinking about that. Not that Mari or Maopa would do anything to harm our bodies. They are more responsible than we would be if the circumstances were reversed."

"Yeah, and as spirits, they at least have an advantage we wouldn't."

"Especially since your grandmother is human, or was at one time."

Dakota snickered. "Knowing Granny, I wouldn't count on that being an advantage. I think she was a wild one in her time, and besides, she doesn't know much about our time."

"Would you please not destroy the security blanket I created?" Yemaya reached over to pull Dakota closer to her. "You know, no matter how much I try, it seems impossible to sink in this lake. I can dive fine, but the moment I want to surface, I do."

"So I've noticed. I suppose it's a built-in safety thing."

"It makes sense. Mari controls all things water. Besides, I doubt if spirits can drown. I wonder..."

Before she could finish the sentence, the Illusionist felt a presence nearby. Looking around, she couldn't find anything out of place. Puzzled, she stood up and walked toward the shore.

"Hey, what's up?" Dakota quickly followed her.

"I feel like we are being watched."

"Here? No one can come here without Mari's permission."

"Normally, I would agree."

Dakota glanced around. "Do you think it's Intunecat? He'd be one to barge in uninvited, I think."

"No. Actually, he would never enter uninvited or unannounced. He seems to have a great respect for Mari, even if he is a little unpredictable."

"That's putting it mildly." Dakota smirked. "Maybe it's just our overactive imaginations. After all, I can't remember us ever fucking like bunnies back home." Wiggling her eyebrows, Dakota pretended to leer at her lover.

"Fucking like bunnies? Where in the world did that come from?" Yemaya laughed and slapped Dakota on the arm. "I do not fuck, sweetie. I wine and dine." Lowering her voice to a low, sultry level, she leaned close to Dakota's ear and whispered, "I caress and stroke. And when you start moaning, I make sure your body comes alive under my hands, my tongue...my touch."

Dakota shivered. Her stomach clenched, causing her to press her hand against it. Whenever Yemaya used that soft, deep, seductive tone, she knew she was going to lose the battle, not that she cared. After all, the Illusionist was a master at making both the world and time disappear, to be replaced by the magical revelation of what true love really felt like.

"Okay, okay. You win!" she gasped. "I was only teasing."

Yemaya gave her a smug smile and ruffled her hair. "But I am not." Her gaze promised more pleasures to come. She spun around suddenly and looked at an empty spot near them. "Whoever you are, show yourself!"

Dakota squinted, trying to see something she couldn't see. "Ummm..."

"Shhhhh. Watch."

Moments later the air shimmered, reminding Dakota of a heat wave. Within seconds, a ghostly figure appeared and solidified.

"I'm beginning to think I've lost my touch." The apparition gave the two humans a sheepish grin. "I was hoping not to intrude on your pleasures."

"Then why did you?"

"To find the answer to a question, nothing more."

"What question?"

"One I need no longer ask. I now have the answer."

"Then as a courtesy, how about telling us what it is."

Dakota listened to the exchange but decided not to join the conversation. Apparently, a battle of wills was taking place between her lover and the ghostly woman.

"The question or the answer?"

Yemaya's eyes narrowed menacingly. Word games always annoyed her. Saira decided to relent.

"I can't give you either," the entity said.

"And I am supposed to accept that?"

"You don't have much choice."

Yemaya didn't say anything. There was something familiar about this entity.

"I know you," she said, her mind racing to remember where they had met.

"No one knows me. Some know of me, though. You are one of those."

"You talk in riddles. I know we have met before."

The apparition gave a slight nod. "Yes, and you'll figure it out without my help, Illusionist."

Yemaya gave a start. Suddenly, images of her minutes in the sarcophagus flooded her mind. "It was you," she said, her voice dropping.

Feeling uncomfortable, Dakota stepped closer to Yemaya and put her hand on her lover's arm.

"What is it?" she whispered. Yemaya gave her a quick glance but immediately turned back to the ghost.

"You have the answer to your question, now," the apparition said, starting to fade.

"Wait!" Yemaya called. "Who are you? At least tell me that."

"It wouldn't give you what you seek. Believe me when I tell you that all will be revealed in time."

Seeing Yemaya's frustration, Dakota stepped forward. "Listen, I don't know what this is about, but I know Yemaya. Unless you give her an answer, she's going to dwell on this for the rest of our vacation and I, frankly, don't think it's very nice of you to barge in and ruin things like this. I don't know who the hell you are, but I would rethink things if I were you. We have connections in high places." Dakota's eyes flashed angrily.

Saira wanted to laugh but refrained.

"You have a champion and fierce defender in this one," she said to Yemaya, motioning toward Dakota. "I'd hate to have her hounding me, so I'll answer some of your questions."

"You interrupted my escape during my performance," Yemaya said.

"Unfortunately, that's true, and it cost you your life."

Dakota stiffened. Yemaya wrapped her arm around her lover and squeezed gently, a signal not to interfere.

"I remember losing consciousness."

"You didn't have time to regain your concentration before you ran out of air. Your lungs ran out of air, and your heart stopped. I had no choice but to intervene. I moved you through time."

"You're a time traveler?"

"That's the simplest way to describe me. Had I not disturbed your concentration, you would have completed your trick without a problem. Since I was the cause of your death, I corrected my mistake by placing you where you were supposed to be. You weren't supposed to feel my presence, but you've clearly inherited some of Mari's gifts."

"You know her?"

The more the apparition talked, the more questions Yemaya had.

"I have said all that I can say. If you think this will ruin your time in this world, I can position you just prior to my arrival. It will not affect me, and you won't remember that I was here."

"No!" Yemaya almost yelled and then repeated the command more softly. "No. Please. At least I know what happened now. That has bothered me since the performance. Thank you."

"I'm truly sorry. I hope you find comfort in what you know and enjoy the rest of your stay here."

"I seriously doubt that's going to happen," Dakota grumbled, suspecting Yemaya was still going to dwell on this for the rest of their stay. "So much for the dream vacation."

"What happens here is totally up to you. Dream well and it will be so."

The apparition vanished, leaving them alone.

"That was frustrating," Dakota said. Her brows furrowed at the thought of Yemaya almost dying. She didn't want to think about that.

Sensing her thoughts, Yemaya grasped Dakota's chin and turned her face up, making eye contact.

"She is right. We can waste the remainder of our time here dwelling on what might have been, or enjoy what little is left doing what we like best."

"And what's that?" Dakota asked, looking very coy. Yemaya was right. They could talk later.

"Fucking like bunnies." The Illusionist grinned, scooped Dakota up, and walked toward their favorite grove.

"Oh, yeah. Works for me."

CHAPTER 1 8

THIS WAS THE STRANGEST voyage Saira had ever taken. The *thread* was thin and knotted like an old wad of twine that balled. Although time wasn't a concern for her, this trip was taking longer than normal. Milliseconds seemed an eternity during her travels.

As she neared her destination, Saira slowed her momentum. Unimaginable power surrounded her, creating a faint sense of vertigo, and confusion.

This isn't good, she thought. Saira had never been lost in time before. Placing her hands against her temples, she concentrated on her surroundings, hoping to recognize something familiar enough to lead her home.

A loud pounding beat rang out incessantly from every direction, its deep pulsations resonating through the very essence of her being. Saira realized she was in serious trouble.

"What you be?" a powerful voice rumbled, its origin rising from the bowels of the dark void surrounding her.

"A traveler," she replied, trying hard to ignore her discomfort as she searched for the voice's source.

"I know no traveler. You no belong. Go way."

"I can't."

Too confused to find the *thread* that would lead her home, and feeling disoriented, she continued to search for a way out.

"Then stay."

"I can't. I'll perish here."

"Then go." The voice sounded disgruntled.

"I don't know the way out."

A sudden heave of energy made Saira fall to her knees and clutch her head in agony. It was the first time she had felt pain. She didn't like it.

"Please," she cried out. "You are destroying me." She could almost feel the mental shrug. Saira felt as though she were dealing with a child. "Do you understand pain?" she gasped.

"Yes. I feel pain. It never go away." There was almost a pout behind the words.

"You're causing me pain. It's new to me," Saira said, hoping the entity was more empathetic than it sounded. "You must stop the pounding."

"Why? Pain good. Pain make me strong. I learn. I grow. One day I will control it instead of feel it."

"I'm not like you. It will destroy me. I'm being torn apart by your continual pounding. I don't have your strength."

The pulsations slowed. Sighing in relief, Saira climbed to her feet.

"Thank you."

"No can I stop. Only slow for short time. I must feed me or die. You go now."

"I wish I could, but I can't find the way out."

"You go!" the voice said angrily. Saira could picture a small child stamping her foot. "I in greater pain. No hold long."

"I'll try to find a *thread* to show me the way out. Please bear with me a little longer."

The resulting sigh would have been comical if the situation weren't so serious.

"I try. Help I get."

"Help?"

There was no response to her question. Saira felt abandoned and knew she was alone. Turning to a bundle of *threads* at her feet, she searched frantically for one that felt familiar, anything that would take her from this place.

CHAPTER 19

MARI WAS ENJOYING her sleep in a perverse sort of way. Dreaming about giant vibrating bunnies chasing her and Maopa would have been amusing had it not been for the leering faces on the toys. Instead, she felt she and Maopa were in dire jeopardy. Wanting to end the dream, Mari struggled to wake up. Before she could arouse herself completely, a weak but familiar voice called to her.

"Mother. You come!"

Mari's forehead wrinkled.

"Daughter?"

"She need help."

"Who needs help?"

"Traveler. She here. No stay. Too much pain, me. Too much pain, her."

"Traveler? Do you mean Saira?"

"No know Saira. Please, Mother. I no hold long. Pain hurt bad. Hurt her. Hurt me."

"Be still, daughter. I'll be there as quickly as I can. You must endure the pain a little longer. Can you do that for me?"

"I try. You hurry?"

"I'll hurry. I promise."

It had been a million years since Mari had visited her firstborn. In the beginning, she spent a lot of time helping in the child's development, but as she grew older, the Earth Mother left her alone to grow at her own pace, much as she had done with many of her children.

* * *

Mari couldn't leave her human body alone without endangering it. She would have to return to the spirit world to get Yemaya to come home.

* * *

Yemaya and Dakota had just finished an especially passionate session of lovemaking. They were reclining on the warm beach, enjoying the cool breeze flowing off the lake. Exhausted but happy, they were startled by Mari's sudden appearance.

"Is it three weeks already?" Dakota asked.

"No, I have an emergency I need to take care of. You need to return to the mortal world. Yemaya's body would be vulnerable to anyone or anything that wanted to take control of her if I left it unattended."

"Can we help you in any way?" Yemaya asked.

"Yes. Tell Maopa that I had to leave. I'll explain once I return. I'm really sorry about this."

"It is fine. We need a break from this vacation." Yemaya chuckled. "We are both exhausted."

"Yeah. It's been fun but a good night's sleep will be heavenly."

"I know the feeling," Mari said. "I must go."

Mari vanished, leaving the two women alone. More tired than normal, they snuggled close, knowing they would soon be home.

* * *

115

Eyes still shut, Yemaya stretched, tensing her muscles until she felt a pop in her neck. Rolling her head slightly from side to side, it took a few seconds for her to realize she was back in her body. Turning on her side, she wrapped an arm around the warm figure next to her and smiled. The scent of Dakota was pleasant, especially with the slightly musky smell of sex mixed in.

I hope it was as good for you as it was for us. The thought was accompanied by a smirk.

"And just what are you smirking about?" Dakota's soft voice whispered next to her cheek.

Yemaya opened her eyes. Sparkling emerald green eyes glinted with a mischievous humor. "Nothing. I was just thinking."

"Uh huh."

"I was...and it was about you." Yemaya gave her a devilish smile.

"And that made you smirk? Doesn't sound too flattering to me."

"Well, actually, about you, Mari and Maopa."

"That's even worse."

"Okay, okay. I was just hoping they had as good a time as we had. Satisfied?"

"Is that normal?" Dakota pulled her head slightly backward and gave her a questioning look. "I mean, thinking of all three of us the moment you wake up?"

"What is this, an inquisition? Where is that sweet girl I was with in the spirit world?"

The arched eyebrow was enough to make Dakota giggle and snuggle closer. "That wasn't a girl, darling. And I'm the only one who should be in your thoughts when you first wake up."

"I see. Would it make you happy if I said you were the very first image that came to mind? Mari and Maopa came afterward, when I realized you smell all warm and musky like you do when we make love. I was just wonder—"

Two hands pushed against her chest, catching the Illusionist by surprise. Dakota rolled over and sat up, looking extremely indignant.

"Are you saying I smell like sex?"

"Well, yes. I noticed it when I woke up. It is quite pleasant."

"That's not the point, and you know it. Granny had *sex* in *my* body!"

"No doubt." Yemaya was amused at her lover's reaction.

"But...but...I need a shower."

Yemaya was unable to contain her laughter and suffered a pillow blow to the head. Grabbing at Dakota, she just missed as Dakota leapt from the bed and ran toward the bathroom, only to find they weren't in her apartment.

"What the hell?"

Looking around, Yemaya realized they were in a hotel room. She slowly climbed out of bed, wandered to the window, and looked out. "I hope you know where we are, because I know nothing about this town."

"Alright, that's it! I'm taking a shower and then we're going to find out what this is about. I only hope they didn't burn down my place," Dakota grumbled and then stomped into the bathroom.

"Not good," Yemaya said. "This is not good at all." Looking up at the ceiling, she shook her head slowly. "I hope you two have a good explanation for this. Otherwise, you are going to be in some very hot water...and I am the one who will pay for it."

Neither Yemaya nor Dakota was happy about putting on the dirty clothes they found lying on the floor next to the bed. To make matters worse, they had trouble buttoning the jeans and pulling up the zippers.

"Don't tell me they shrank our clothes." Dakota, frustrated at not being able to push the jeans button in, threw her hands

117

in the air. "I give up." She pulled her tank top on and left it draped outside of her pants, hoping it was long enough to hide the open vee below her navel and the slightly protruding belly. "They must have eaten like little piggies," she grumped, slapping her stomach unhappily.

Yemaya felt her lover's frustration as she, too, had difficulty pushing the button through the hole. Only determination brought victory, and then she regretted her success. The tightness cutting into her waist fell just short of being painful. "This is one time I wish I were a magician instead of an illusionist."

"Me too. Making this fat go away isn't my idea of fun. Let's go see what else they've been up to."

"Well, they obviously enjoyed the food while they were here. Maybe the hotel was is just a part of experiencing this world."

"Uh huh. Let's hope."

They took the elevator to the first floor and approached the checkout counter. The receptionist gave them a friendly smile.

"Ms. Lysanne, Ms. Devereaux, you're up early today. Your new room isn't ready yet, but if you can come back in an hour, I'll get housekeeping right on it."

"New room?" Dakota asked.

"You still want a different room, right?"

Yemaya pulled Dakota aside. "It might be a good idea to keep the reservation until we find out what is going on. There must be something wrong with the room we are in."

"Or the apartment...but, you're right. Better safe than sorry." Turning back to the receptionist, Dakota gave her a pained smile.

"Of course, thank you. I hope you get the problem in our other room taken care of."

"Problem? Was something not to your liking?"

"Nooo. Everything was fine. Ummm...I'm getting a little forgetful, I guess. Exactly why are we switching rooms?"

"Ms. Devereaux." The receptionist laughed. "You're such a tease, and you've been pulling my leg all along, haven't you? I mean with that country folk accent. I knew it couldn't be real. No one talks like that nowadays."

"Oh, shore nuff. I was funnin' yah," Dakota replied, trying to mimic her granny.

"Well, you're pretty good at it. I bet my manager you were faking it. She said you might be from West Virginia, but I knew better. No one writes like you and then speaks that way."

"True. Now, about the room."

"Right. Today it will be 227. Tomorrow 318 and then 129. It's getting to be quite a game for the housekeepers to get them ready in time for you two. They have a contest going to see who can clean your new room the fastest. Thankfully, you normally sleep in late so there really hasn't been much of a rush."

Stunned by the information, the two women stared at the receptionist, unable to say anything. Finally, Yemaya realized someone needed to say something. "I think we need to go for a walk. Is there any place we can get a good breakfast?"

"You mean other than the pizza place and hotdog stands?"

"Pizza...hot...ummm...yes. I think we would like a normal breakfast today."

"Well, there's Benny's. It's right across from that toy shop you went to yesterday."

"Ta...toy shop?" Dakota stammered.

"Yeah. You know...Tango's Ticklers. Are you feeling okay, Ms. Devereaux? You have a funny look on your face."

"Oh, sure. I'm just wonderful."

Yemaya knew Dakota was about to lose it. Patting her arm sympathetically, she winked at the hotel clerk. "She needs something to eat and then some quiet time. Family matters. You know how trying that can be."

"Gee, I'm sorry. I hope it's nothing serious."

"Not at the moment, but I suspect it will get worse before it gets better. Would you mind giving us directions to the restaurant? I think we may have gotten a little confused yesterday."

"Sure. When you leave, go around the corner to the right for a block, then turn left. Two blocks down on the right. You can't miss it."

"Thank you."

Taking Dakota's arm, Yemaya pulled her out the main door and turned right. A few minutes later, they walked into Benny's and sat down. Neither spoke during the short walk.

"Are you alright?" Yemaya asked.

"I think so. Just a bit overwhelmed...and wondering about the apartment. And I don't even want to think about Granny and Mari doing the dirty with our bodies."

"How about we get something to eat then check out your place? We can deal with those two later."

The food was hot and savory. Scrambled eggs covered with chili and cheese, hot biscuits, and several cups of coffee helped to mellow some of the tension.

"Guess we might as well go look at the damage," Dakota said pessimistically.

Squeezing her hand, Yemaya hoped things weren't as bad as Dakota imagined. With her jeans cutting painfully into her waist, she was beginning to feel the same pessimism.

Flagging a taxi, they gave the cabbie the address and then sat quietly staring out the windows, each wondering what other surprises lay ahead. Thirty minutes later, they hesitantly entered the apartment. Surprisingly, the living room was in decent shape, giving them hope. The kitchen? Well, it could have been worse—not much—but still. The refrigerator was empty except for a jar of dill pickles, some olives, two bottles of Lime-aid, and some leftovers that looked disgustingly familiar.

"Looks like they cleaned us out," Dakota said.

"At least we can start fresh. I hate to think what two weeks of old food would taste like."

"You did notice they didn't touch the leftovers? That's what it looks like...tasting is out of the question."

"Like I said."

"Let's check the bedroom," Dakota said.

They pushed open the door, stepped inside, and stopped. Silence. It was the ominous type that always preceded a storm.

"My...bed. What happened to my bed?" Dakota walked over to stand next to the box spring with no mattress.

"I am not sure I want to know," Yemaya said as a thought slowly took form, "but I think I have an idea."

She walked to the linen closet and opened the door. Several empty shelves stared back at her. *I hope I am wrong about the clothes.* Pulling open several dresser drawers, all Yemaya could do was shake her head and try not to laugh out loud. "I hope you are up for a day of shopping."

"What?"

Dakota ran to the dresser and stared hopelessly at the emptiness.

"Where's my underwear? Where are my linens?"

"I think Mari and Maopa threw them out. Spirits have no need of clothing so they would not know about washers and dryers."

"Damn. How could they go through so much in such a short time? And what about your stuff?"

Yemaya walked to one of her suitcases, opened the lid, and smiled. "I guess they wanted to use yours first. Mine are here."

"Well, if you think you're going to get off lightly, forget it. We're going shopping together."

"You know, sweetie, this may not be such a bad thing. After all, you might have a little trouble fitting into the ones you had...at least until you lose a few pounds."

The look Dakota gave her would have killed any normal mortal. Chuckling, Yemaya wrapped her arms around her lover and hugged her. "My clothes will probably be tight too. A few extra strolls around the neighborhood and we will be back to normal."

"You might be. I don't lose weight so easily."

"You exaggerate."

"Like hell. I don't want to hear anymore. Let's go."

Deciding discretion was the better part of valor, Yemaya merely nodded.

The streets were crowded as people moved about their business. The two women walked the few blocks to a local department store. Neither noticed the street vendor until they had almost passed him.

"Hey, Ms. Lysanne, Ms. Devereaux," he called. Yemaya and Dakota stopped. When he motioned them over, they hesitated and shrugged simultaneously.

"What now?" Dakota muttered.

"Here yah go, ladies. Two of the finest dogs you ever ate, and I know how much you like them."

"Uh...Thanks, but we're really not hungry," Dakota said.

"Not hungry? You're always hungry. I've never seen two women eat so many dogs in my life. Why even my wife didn't believe me until she came down the other day and saw you."

"Oh God."

"Are you two feeling okay? You've been eating my dogs almost every day."

"Every day?" Yemaya asked.

"Sure, sometimes twice."

Dakota groaned. "Twice? No wonder I'm so friggin' fat."

After giving her a curious look, the vendor turned to Yemaya. "Is she okay?"

"She has been better. Look. We forgot to bring money with us today," Yemaya said, trying to think of some way to get out of the situation.

"You two are so funny. Go on. Eat up."

Normally an avid hotdog lover, the thought of eating one now disgusted Dakota. Glancing down at the slightly bulging tummy peeking over her waistband, she glared at the offending object in the man's hand and stalked off.

"Gosh. Is it something I said?"

Yemaya looked wistfully at the hotdog in his hand.

"No, she is having a bad day. Maybe tomorrow we can come back. They do look good."

Walking off, Yemaya caught up with Dakota, glanced at her face, and grinned. *Passing up two hotdogs? Disappointing. Dakota's expression? Priceless.*

CHAPTER 2 0

MAOPA WASN'T SURE what was happening. One moment she was curled up against Mari's warm body, and the next she was in the spirit world, alone. Even Yemaya and Dakota had disappeared.

"Dagnabit. That woman better be havin' a good explanation fer leavin' me here alone."

Not wanting to stay there by herself, she returned to the Eternal Fire to check on the other spirits. It had been awhile since she had seen them.

Sarpe, the serpent spirit, lay coiled next to a log, her body relaxed, her eyes closed. Arbora, the woodland spirit, was talking to Ursa, the bear spirit. The two were bonded, although they seemed an odd couple. Arbora was small and slender with lavender eyes. Her green and purple hair looked like a wild bush reaching toward the sky. Ursa was huge and hairy, closely resembling a large grizzly. Only the eyes were different. Pale yellow, they glowed when the flames from the fire reflected across the black pupils.

Turning at Maopa's appearance, Arbora jumped up and gave her a quick hug. "It's been a long time."

"Mari and I be gettin' to know each other better."

"It's about time. She's been alone too long."

"Yep. I figgered that."

"So, where is she?"

"Now that be somethin' I'd like ta know mahself. One minute we was all snuggled up, the next she be gone."

"She does that sometimes."

"Well, this time be diff'rent. Yemaya and Dakota done vanished too."

"Really? Let's see if we can find them."

Arbora moved to the fire and passed her hand through the dancing flames. Immediately a picture appeared, showing Yemaya and Dakota talking to the hotel receptionist.

"I'll be danged. They done went back. That Mari, I bet she's done tarred of bein' human."

"And I bet there's a good story behind that comment." Arbora's lips curled up slightly.

"Shore nuff. Only don't go expectin' me ta tell it. She'd not be appreeshiatin' me jabberin' behind her back."

"Oh, we'll wait. It'll be more fun with her present."

"That be true. It'd serve her right, leavin' me alone like that."

Glancing toward Sarpe, Maopa leaned close to Arbora to whisper a question. "What be wrong with Sarpe, there? She's lookin' a bit puny."

"She's tired. Her last trip to the mortal world really affected her energy level," Arbora whispered, "She's got a girlfriend, but isn't talking."

"Playin' it real secretive, eh? That be good news if'n she do gots her one. Now, if only Mari'd show up. Ain't like her to be gone like this."

"I'm sure she'll be back soon. In the meantime, let's go pick on Ursa. She's feeling a little grumpy."

"Can't be havin' that now, can we?" Maopa chuckled, trying to recall a time when the bear spirit wasn't grumpy.

CHAPTER 21

MARI REACHED HER destination in less than a minute. During the short journey, she noticed the deep pulsations had slowed to less than a million beats per second.

"This isn't good," she muttered. "Daughter, are you okay?"

"Hurry, Mother. I hurt."

Mari could feel her child's pain. Her daughter had grown stronger in the past five billion years, making it more difficult to ease her discomfort. "I'm here."

The sigh of relief was audible. "Take away. She die soon."

It was true. No one but the Earth Mother could withstand the beat of her daughter's life force for long, even at the decreased rate.

"I'll see what I can do. Can you hold on a little longer?"

"I try, but soon beat must grow. Not good to keep slow. I grow weaker. Many die. I die."

"I know. Please, keep it low as long as you can." Approaching Saira, Mari was surprised the apparition couldn't feel her presence. Apparently, something was terribly wrong. "Saira?"

Saira searched the darkness, trying to locate the spirit. "Mari? Is that you? I can't see anything."

"Nothing can see in this place. What are you doing here?"

"I followed a *thread*, but lost it."

"A *thread*? You mean one of my *threads*."

"Yes. I should have known now wasn't the right time."

"Why?"

"It was too weak. Weak *threads* are fragile."

"Did it break?"

"I don't know. Possibly. I've never been lost before. It frightens me to know this happened."

"I can imagine. The energy here is stronger than anything you could have ever encountered. My daughter has reduced its effects, but she can't sustain this level for long. We must get you out of here before her strength is depleted."

"I've tried, but I can't find the right *thread*. They all look alike."

"For good reason. Life began here. It's the birthplace of everything on this world. But, we can discuss that later. We need to find that *thread*."

"Maybe I can follow you out."

"I don't think so. I need nothing to guide me here. What exactly are you looking for?"

"The end of the *thread* that led me here. There are so many though." Running her hands around the giant ball, Saira grew more frustrated. "They all look alike."

Mari tried to decipher minute differences in the *threads* but found none. There was no end or beginning to any of them. Time was running out.

"Daughter, can you help us?"

"Yes, Mother. I help. What you want of me?"

"The Traveler. She needs to return the way she came. Do you know what brought her here?"

"No."

"She followed one of the strings in your ball of life. A special one that will lead her to my home. Will you try to find it for me?"

"I try. I try."

Time slowed to a crawl as the two entities waited. Saira felt slightly better since the pounding had eased, but she knew it was at the expense of Mari's child.

"If she doesn't find it soon," Mari said, "you'll have to choose one and take your chances."

"I'll do what I must before jeopardizing your daughter's life. If I fail to find my way home, then so be it."

"I suspect failure may be more catastrophic than you think, Saira. It's imperative you arrive in the present as quickly as possible."

"I find, Mother! I find!" the voice said joyfully.

"Where?"

Mari and Saira searched the massive ball for the *thread* but didn't see anything different.

"We can't see it. Can you try a little harder to show us?" Mari said.

The tip of a small string-like object wiggled frantically, desperate to attract their attention.

"You see? You see?"

"Yes, we see it."

"Traveler go now?"

"Yes, Traveler go now. You've done well, daughter. I'm proud of you."

Turning to Saira, Mari pointed to the tiny object moving rapidly back and forth. "Go."

"Thank you, Mari." Totally out of character, Saira hugged Mari and then grasped the *thread*. Immediately, she felt a familiar tug.

"Thank you, Gaia!" she called out.

"Bye, Traveler, bye," the voice replied, saddened by the apparition's departure.

A powerful surge sent Saira speeding on her way to the present. The heartbeat of the planet resumed its normal pace.

"You're growing up. Soon, you'll be able to control everything at will. Have you thought about what you'll be able to do then?" Mari asked her first born.

"I think, Mother. I not know. It seem far away still."

"You have plenty of time to plan ahead, daughter. When the time's right, you'll make the right choices...just as you did now."

Mari could feel her child swelling with pride, and she smiled. "You're my first born, Gaia. You will always be my favorite."

"You too," Gaia said and beamed.

It was such a childish response, but Mari was happy. "I must go, but you know I'm always near if you need me."

"I know. I happy you come. Happy Traveler safe. She nice. Will I see her again?"

"I think so, when the time is right. Now that you know what she needs, you'll be able to guide her home."

"You tell Traveler, she come anytime. Short stay, though. I not like pain."

"I'll tell her. I'm sure you two will have lots to talk about."

"Yes. I like talk."

Mari was about to leave when she felt a warmth encircle her. "Mother?"

"What, daughter?"

"I love you."

"I love you too. Be happy, and call to me if you ever need me."

"I call."

Mari sensed Gaia wanted to ask her something, but was reluctant to take up any more of her time.

"Is there something else you want or need?"

"Many questions I have. Can you stay longer?"

Nodding, the Earth Mother slid down next to the *threads* of life and made herself comfortable. Gaia had evolved to a sentient level. She needed not only guidance, but the emotional stability only a mother could offer...not to mention company. The time had come for her to provide both. Unknowingly, Saira had once again affected the life of someone she came in contact with. Mari's future was becoming more interesting and a lot more complicated.

After hours of chatting, Mari finally stood.

"I'm sorry. I do have to leave now. Will you be okay?" she asked, caressing the stone walls with her hand.

"I fine. It nice we talk. Will you come soon back?"

"Yes. I've left you alone for far too long. It was inexcusable. I'm going to come here at least once a week so we can chat. I may not be able to stay long, though." An overwhelming joy surrounded Mari. The ground began shaking.

"I happy. Thank you."

"You're welcome, Gaia. Bye, now."

"Bye, Mother, bye, bye. Love you."

"I love you."

Returning home, Mari listened patiently to Maopa's lecture and then apologized for her thoughtlessness. Afterward, she told everyone about the predicament Saira had gotten into, leaving out most of her conversation with Gaia.

CHAPTER 2 2

YEMAYA AND DAKOTA finished shopping at the Bed, Buttons and Bath. Victoria's Secret was next on the list to check out the underwear selection. After regaining her sense of humor, Dakota started to tease Yemaya.

"You can laugh all you want, but you're going to have to be a real magician to make that tummy disappear."

"Are you saying I picked the wrong occupation?" The Illusionist laughed and ruffled Dakota's hair.

"Naw. You might want to think about expanding your horizons, though. Oh wait! You already have."

Giving Yemaya a wicked grin, Dakota took off running, knowing she would pay for her remark later. When she realized she wasn't being chased, she looked back. Yemaya was standing next to a newsstand, staring at a row of magazines. "Hey, what's up?" she asked, walking back to see what had attracted her partner's attention.

The front page of a popular sleazy tabloid displayed a photo of two women sitting on a park bench with their arms wrapped around each other. The headlines read, "Illusionist Makes Magic in City Park." The article described how Yemaya Lysanne was cuddling with an unknown woman.

Yemaya's rigid body spoke volumes. "Looks like our bodysitters don't know about the paparazzi," Dakota said. "It's a cute picture in a bizarre sort of way. I mean, knowing that's us, but it isn't."

Yemaya didn't move or respond. All she did was stare at the photo, unable to voice her thoughts.

"Listen, sweetie, I know you don't like publicity, especially this type, but it'll blow over in a week. Trust me, I'm in the business." Silence. "At least they recognized you. I'm just the 'unknown woman' in the picture."

Dakota could almost feel the drop in temperature when Yemaya turned icy blue eyes in her direction. *Uh oh. This isn't good.*

"Okay, it's tacky, but who really pays attention to tabloids? Everyone knows they're crap, and besides, the picture doesn't even look like you." The Illusionist didn't blink. She just stared at Dakota, her jaw clenched, muscles flexing as teeth ground silently together.

"All right then, you stay here and think about how you're going to kill the photographer. I need underwear...badly. I'll be back in a while."

Exasperated, Dakota stalked off, knowing things didn't bode well for the rest of the day. She had almost made it to Victoria's Secret when she felt a presence behind her. Turning around, she nearly bumped into Yemaya, who had silently followed her.

"Look, if you're going to give me the silent treatment because of your ancestor's irresponsible behavior, then you can wait out here."

"*My* ancestor's?" Yemaya growled, grinding her teeth.

"You're the one that attracts all the attention...at least, the photographer thought it was you. He sure didn't take that photo because of me. I don't have a fan club or news people chasing after me to get a story."

"Are you blaming me for this? It was your granny that was sharing that park bench."

"Oh, right. Blame Granny. Like she'd really know anything about sleazy photographers."

"I am not blaming anyone. You started this."

"So now it's my fault you gave me the cold shoulder?"

"I did not give you the cold shoulder. I was thinking."

"Well, it sure looked and felt like it. Cripeez! You didn't even notice the way people were going out of their way to avoid you. I know you hate this type of trash, but in your line of work, it's going to happen. You can't hide from prying eyes no matter how much you want to. I'm surprised you've kept your life as private as you have."

"It is not about the picture."

"Then what is this about?"

Yemaya glanced down at her feet, avoiding eye contact. "I do not *cuddle*."

Her voice was so low, Dakota barely heard the words. "Excuse me?"

"You heard me."

"Yeah, but I can't believe all of this is about *cuddling*." Dakota found it difficult to keep a straight face, let alone hold in her laughter. Yemaya gave her an indignant look and stalked past her into the store. *Conversation closed.*

Chuckling, Dakota followed. "Oh boy. If that isn't an image buster," she muttered under her breath. "Note to self. Never use the word *cuddle* around her."

* * *

Dakota was doing her best to ignore Yemaya's restless prowling around the small apartment. The shopping spree was successful even though the conversation had dwindled to almost nothing. The new sheets, towels, and underwear were safely tucked away in their appropriate spaces.

Yemaya wasn't happy. Privacy was important to her. The tabloid photo of her and Dakota caught her by surprise, but the word *cuddling* was embarrassing. Once news of the article reached her friends and family, she would be teased unmercifully.

She didn't realize just how quickly rumors spread until her cell phone rang. "Lysanne," she answered curtly.

"Well, sister, it appears you've finally made it to the big time. The front page of National Exposure is quite an accomplishment."

"Did you call me to discuss this, or is there something else on your mind?" Yemaya said coldly.

"Can't a loving brother give his sister a call now and then without you looking for ulterior motives?"

Yemaya could hear the barely suppressed laughter in Raidon's voice. The sound of a male giggling in the background didn't do anything to improve her mood.

"Any brother but you. And tell Reymone I can hear him. That will not bode well for him when I get home."

"Yemaya, I'm shocked. Threatening my lover? Tch, tch."

"Why are you calling, Raidon?"

"I was worried about you. When I heard about the photo, I couldn't believe it was you. My big sister would never be caught doing something so intimate in public. *Cuddling*. That sounds so...cute. And with the picture on the Internet, it's definitely going to ruin that aloof image you've managed to maintain all these years."

"Internet? Someone posted that on the net?"

"Of course. You, my dear, are big news. Websites are popping up all over the place, speculating on your relationship with this 'unknown' woman. You now have an 'official' website asking for more photos and information about you and your mystery woman."

"Damn those two," Yemaya muttered, wondering how hard it was to kill spirits.

"Those two? You know who's behind all of this?"

"No. At least not as far as the Internet postings, but I sure as hell can find out who this photographer is and make his life miserable."

"Don't do anything drastic. It'll only cause you more heartburn."

"I really do not care if I spontaneously combust. This man will regret the day he bought his first camera."

"Really, sis, you can't put all the blame on someone who took advantage of a good opportunity."

"Maybe not, but I sure can make him think twice about screwing around with people's lives."

"I've never known you to be vindictive. Is there something you should be telling me?"

"No. I—"

The cell phone clicked twice to let her know another caller was trying to reach her. "Hold on, Raidon. I have another call."

Yemaya switched to the second caller and tried not to sound so irritated. "Lysanne."

"Yemaya, have you seen the National Exposure yet?"

"Yes, Sonny, I have. Apparently everyone else has too."

"Wonderful! You won't believe the calls I'm getting. Everyone wants to know if you're gay and who the mystery woman is."

Yemaya's voice lowered to a throaty growl. "And what makes having the entire world chasing after me so great?"

"Publicity. What else? I've received four offers to fund your next six shows. You could make millions if you play this right."

"I do not need more money, Sonny. I need privacy."

"Good luck on that," Sonny replied cheerfully. "By the way, what does Dakota have to say about being the 'mystery woman'?"

"Nothing. I will talk to you later, Sonny. Raidon is on the other line. If anyone calls to ask about this, hang up."

"But, —"

"I said hang up. And keep Dakota's name out of this, or I will find myself an agent who can follow orders."

"Oh, don't go getting all ballistic on me, Yemaya. We both know you won't replace me. I'm too good at what I do. Say hi to Raidon, and give my regards to Dakota."

A click of the line told her he had hung up. She switched back to Raidon. "Are you still there?"

"I thought you'd forgotten me."

"As if. Is there anything else we need to talk about?"

"You know Yemaya, your sense of humor is sorely lacking. I hope you don't talk to Dakota the way you do to me. Hold on. Reymone wants to talk to you."

"Hey, Yem, how are you doing?" her brother's partner asked cheerfully.

"As well as can be expected. How are you?"

"If I could get this brother of yours to lighten up some, I'd be a lot better. He's such a stick-in-the-mud."

"Tell me about it."

Yemaya was extremely fond of Reymone. He was the light to her brother's darkness, and neither was afraid to discuss Raidon in his presence. A loud snort in the background told Yemaya that her brother had heard her remark.

"Do you need something?" she asked.

"Not really. I wanted to make sure you and Daks are okay."

"We are fine. Dakota says it will blow over in a few days. I hope so."

"I agree with her. With all the crap going on in the world, your fifteen minutes of fame will be short-lived, I'm sure."

"Thanks, Reymone. Look, I need to go. Say good-bye to Raidon for me, and tell him his turn will come."

"Sure thing. Yemaya, I really think you and Dakota need to take some time off. You've been pushing yourself a lot in the past few months. A short vacation wouldn't hurt, you know?"

Yemaya rolled her eyes. "Right," she said and hung up. "If you only knew," she muttered.

CHAPTER 2 3

FOR THE FIRST TIME in her existence, Saira's self-confidence was badly bruised. Her journey to the heart of the planet had left her shaken. Self-doubt plagued her thoughts even as a new tug demanded her attention.

Saira needed counsel, but didn't know who to turn to. Mari was her first choice, but she had already jeopardized the safety of her child. The Twin was neither attainable nor someone she was interested in meeting at this time. Why she even thought of him she didn't know.

Dis was out of the question. His primary interests were his lust and keeping order in the Underworld. Saira knew he would soon have his hands full. Caelene was ambitious and powerful. How powerful, Dis couldn't even imagine.

That left Intunecat. Of all the entities she had met, he was the least approachable, but seemed one of the wisest. Perhaps even more so than Mari.

Intunecat was recovering from his visit to Lilith. Trips to the mortal world were exhausting at best, even for one as powerful as he. Intunecat enjoyed his chats with Lilith, however. This one was no different.

Confident that his sanctuary was safe, he relaxed in his favorite chair and watched the images of Yemaya and Dakota sitting in an old theater watching a movie. Intunecat was aware that Mari and Maopa inhabited their bodies. He chuckled at the thought of the two mortals finding out what the two spirits were doing.

Then the images wavered. Something or someone was disturbing the balance of darkness in his realm. *Not again.* Before he had time to scan its boundaries, Saira shimmered into view and then solidified in front of him.

"You!"

Saira recognized the frustration in Intunecat's voice. "I'm sorry to intrude like this. I need to talk to you."

"We already talked. You weren't supposed to come back, at least not this soon," he said. "Don't tell me you have more questions."

"Yes...no...I don't know."

Intunecat could feel her confusion and motioned for her to sit. "What's bothering you, Saira?"

"I'm afraid."

Those two words told the dark spirit everything he needed to know, except the cause of her fear. "Of what?"

"Getting lost. I'm afraid I'll become lost in the web if I continue my quests."

"After all these eons, you actually think you could get lost? Why now?"

Saira hesitated and then told him about her quest to find Gaia. Intunecat listened patiently.

"You found your way back to the present. Gaia is sentient enough to prevent a recurrence should you wish to try that again."

"Yes, but she's young. I may not be so lucky the next time. If it happened once, it can happen again."

"Well, if it does, which I seriously doubt, you will find your way forward. It's what you do. I would think any *thread* will take you to another you'll recognize."

"It doesn't work that way," Saira said. "I can only return on the strands that are intertwined with the lives I followed. I don't necessarily need to return on the same one, but I must return on one that is directly connected to the time and life I sought."

"Are you so sure of that? Have you ever tried following an unknown strand?"

"No. It's not my nature."

"Saira. We don't always know what our true nature is until we are tested by something. You will never know if you never try."

"This is the one thing I'm sure about. It's hard to explain, but I know I can't go beyond that which isn't connected in some way to my initial calling."

"My dear, survival is the best reason to try something different, even if it seems suicidal. I hope you never have to make such a choice, but don't be afraid to do it if you need to."

Saira looked down at her clasped hands. "I'll try," she said.

"Good. Now, perhaps you will satisfy my curiosity. Why come to me about this? I can no more travel into the past than you can into the future."

Saira shrugged. "I needed someone to talk to. You were the logical choice."

"That's debatable, but what makes you say that?"

Saira hesitated, not sure how much she should disclose. Sensing her unease, Intunecat rose from his chair and paced back and forth, searching for a way to help her through her dilemma.

"Saira, why did you come here? Why me?" he asked again.

Taking a deep breath, which Intunecat found amusing considering she didn't require air, Saira spoke. "You are First Born. You have knowledge and wisdom beyond anything the others could ever imagine."

"You give me too much credit. I may have knowledge, but even I would argue the wisdom part. Besides, my expertise doesn't include time travel. Neither do the other First Born possess such knowledge." Kneeling beside her, Intunecat picked up Saira's hands and turned the palms up. Running his thumbs gently across the skin, he was amazed at how soft and warm they felt, considering she didn't have a physical body.

"Listen to me, Traveler. Each of us is unique. Mari is the Earth Mother. Her world is one of light, beauty and color. It's filled with life and death, and constantly changing. Then there's the Twin. He stays locked away in a realm very few are allowed to enter. What he feels or thinks only he knows. Some believe him to be loving, while others fear his wrath. He does little to resolve the debate and is a mystery to everyone, except perhaps Dis.

The Underlord probably knows his Twin better than anyone. Perhaps that's why they're always at odds. When you know someone too well, you know their strengths and their weaknesses. Dis loves life, but he loves it selfishly. He thinks mostly about his personal pleasures, although he seems to have a weak spot for Lilith. She is perhaps the closest he ever came to feeling true love. Unfortunately, he squandered that opportunity a long time ago. Too bad. Lilith is an amazing woman. Strong, powerful, independent. His loss is the mortal world's gain."

"And you?" Saira asked softly, looking down at the hands gently holding hers.

"Me? I'm the master of darkness. It's a realm where little can exist except for short periods. My world is void of color and light. Only I can appreciate the beauty within. I feel its softness. It's warm like velvet...no, softer than the softest velvet anyone can ever imagine. I hear music where there is none, notes drifting randomly through the darkness. joining in a moment of harmony that never repeats itself. Every second is filled with a richness that makes my very essence vibrate with unimaginable power. The darkness and I are one. I'm happy here, and yet, I'm not. Do you understand what I'm saying?"

"I'm not sure."

He pulled Saira to her feet, turned her toward the darkness, and waved his hand. For a moment, Saira experienced everything Intunecat had just described. It was both overwhelming and magnificent. From behind her, she felt his warm breath as he whispered near her ear.

"We're the guardians of our own worlds, Saira. I, the darkness. Mari, the light. Dis, the Underworld. And the Twin, the Overworld. Without us, each realm would be chaos, and without each realm, the other worlds could not exist. We're the balance to all that ever was and ever will be."

"Yes, I can see that. But what does that have to do with me?"

"Everything, my dear, and maybe nothing. What's the one thing all of us have in common, the one thing even First Born can't control?"

"You mean time?"

Intunecat nodded. "Time. First Born have never mastered time. Only you can do that."

"I don't master time. I'm only a Traveler."

"If you say so. Still, I find it interesting that only you can travel the web. For all our powers, we're incapable of such journeys. We didn't even know it was possible until recently. Don't you find that a little strange?"

"I've never really thought about it."

"Then perhaps you should. There's a purpose behind all things. For some unknown reason, you have this unique ability to go back and forth along these *threads*. Have you ever thought about what happens to these strands as time moves forward?"

"Not really. The future is beyond me."

"Exactly, but it does exist even if it isn't attainable. You were the one who described time as a giant web, constantly growing larger and more complicated. If you're right, then logic dictates that the bigger it grows, the more stress it puts on each strand before and behind it. What happens if one of those *threads* breaks?"

"I don't know. Probably nothing. Or maybe the web would unravel and time would cease to exist. Who's to say it hasn't already happened?"

"True. There are infinite possibilities. What if, and I'm merely posing a theory, what if someone could journey into the past to make sure each strand remained intact? If a *thread* is created when one life intersects another, wouldn't it be reasonable to believe that a new one is created or an old one strengthened every time you make your journey?"

Saira had never given much thought to there being a purpose for her trips into the past. For her, it was simply a matter of looking for answers. If Intunecat's theory was accurate, it put a tremendous responsibility on her shoulders. It was a burden she wasn't sure she had the courage to carry.

"If what you say is possible, then I'm more afraid than ever. Were I to get lost I might never find the weakened *threads*."

"If you never take the journey, you'll never strengthen them either. Of course, all this is speculation. There's no way to prove or disprove any of it."

"True." In a way, Saira hoped he was wrong. But, what if?

"But, what if?" Intunecat asked, as if reading her thoughts. "Isn't it better to take the chance and possibly fail than to not take it, knowing you will fail?"

"If it were only that simple."

Realizing that in telling her his theory, he had placed an unimaginable burden on Saira, Intunecat regretted speaking so freely. Now wasn't the right time for her to seek the meaning of her own existence.

"Saira. you once told me you had free will to choose whether you follow a *thread*, even though you felt compelled to do so. Nothing has changed. I know you're afraid. Fear can be a good thing. It makes you more cautious. Personally, I think you have nothing more to be afraid of. Talk to others. I'm sure you'll get a half dozen more theories that are equally plausible."

Saira stared blindly into the darkness. "You are probably right, Intunecat. I'm over-thinking everything."

"My point exactly. Besides, you have one thing going for you that you've never had before."

"And that would be?"

"Me." The Dark One grinned. "If I'm to get any peace and quiet here, I'm going to have to keep an eye on you."

Saira laughed. She was really starting to like this First Born. Intunecat had a way of putting everything in perspective.

"And what could you do? You're the first to admit you can't come and get me."

"Ah. Well, that's a question that only needs to be answered if it happens. Until then, let's not think about it."

"Agreed. Thank you, Intunecat. You are kind to have listened to me."

"My pleasure. Now, if you don't mind, would you please give me a little warning before you barge in again? It is quite disconcerting having you females coming and going at your leisure."

"You have my word, although I can't say how much notice I can give. Perhaps you should install a doorbell. I must go. Someone's calling me."

"Doorbell?" Intunecat asked. "This, from a ghost." He rolled his eyes dramatically. Before he could say anything else, Saira leaned over, gave him a quick kiss on the cheek, and disappeared.

Stunned, Intunecat stood still for several seconds and then raised his hand to the spot her lips had touched. The area was pleasantly warm. "What is it about females that makes them so..."

A good, descriptive word escaped him.

143

CHAPTER 2 4

BINKY CARLLETON WAS in his glory. The snapshot of the Illusionist making out in the park had made him a thousand bucks and given him instant notoriety. Several magazines had contacted him, offering more money if he could furnish more pictures. To make things even better, he received an anonymous tip that Ms. Lysanne was going to be at the park around 6 p.m. with her mysterious girlfriend.

At 5:45, Binky positioned himself behind some shrubbery and waited. Nervously, he checked the settings on his camera, knowing he would only have a few seconds to snap some pictures. Minutes later, his subject strolled down the sidewalk with her arm wrapped around a shorter blonde.

"This is great," he muttered, already thinking about how he would spend the money he was going to get.

When they sat down on the same bench as in the original photo and started kissing, Binky adjusted the focus and snapped two shots. Several people strolled by, glanced at the two women, and smiled before continuing on their way. One woman noticed the cameraman and frowned.

"Paparazzi," she said, disgustedly. She walked to where he was hiding, stood between him and his subjects, and pointed her finger accusingly. "You should be ashamed of yourself, young man. Spying on people is rude. What would your mother think?"

Realizing he was busted, Binky decided to leave. Scurrying off, he kept his head down in case anyone else was looking. Had he looked back he would have seen a pair of green eyes and a pair of icy blue ones following his furtive movements as he disappeared into a small crowd.

"I figger he done got what he needs."

"Looks like it. Now, he'll get what he deserves. Let's go home. Yemaya and Dakota will take it from here."

Anxious to develop the two photos, Binky rushed back to his apartment. At the entrance, several people were milling around, some looking at photos they were holding. As he approached, a woman dressed in a green jacket and khaki slacks looked up and pointed at him.

"There he is!" she yelled.

Surprised, Binky stopped and stared at the group. Cameras appeared and the familiar click of the shutters chattered ominously. Unsure of himself, he pushed past them and disappeared into the building.

"That's weird," he said aloud to himself.

A small photo lab had been set up in his spare bedroom. He unloaded the camera and began the slow process of developing the film. Fifteen minutes later, he stared in satisfaction at the prints hanging on the clothesline.

"The papers are going to love this."

Later, after sliding the dry photos into a brown folder, he put on a light jacket and left his apartment. At the front door, he was met again with the sound of cameras clicking and a few flashes.

"Are you the guy who took the pictures of the Illusionist?" asked a man holding a microphone.

"Yeah, that's me. Why?"

"You're famous now," another man said.

Suddenly feeling important, Binky grinned and posed for a few more pictures. When new photographers appeared, he frowned and hurried away.

This is crazy, he thought.

Twenty minutes later, he was walking toward the entrance of the National Exposure when he noticed another group of photographers by the main entrance. Ducking his head, he tried to sneak past them but found it impossible. The familiar clicking was getting annoying.

When he finally managed to get inside, the secretary of the editor-in-chief motioned for him to follow her. Leading him to Larry Dunbar's office, she knocked once on the door and then opened it.

"He's here, Mr. Dunbar."

"Show him in," a deep voice said.

She signaled for Binky to enter and quietly shut the door behind him.

Larry Dunbar was a short, balding man in his sixties. As editor-in-chief of the National Exposure for fifteen years, he enjoyed the power of his position. Few people dared to challenge him, and those who did were usually subjected to a form of harassment that proved effective, but wasn't illegal.

Dunbar would send the paparazzi to hound them, their family, and friends. No place was safe or sacred. Soon, the constant attention became unbearable. His enemies would give up and call a truce. Dunbar gloried in his victories, knowing he had the power of the press behind him. Today, he wasn't very happy.

"You see those assholes outside?" he asked angrily.

"Yeah. I guess I'm famous, huh?" Binky said, smiling smugly.

"Famous my ass. They aren't interested in you. They're after me."

"Well, they certainly were interested in me at my apartment and when I arrived here."

"Those assholes have been following me around for two days. Everywhere I go, there are people taking pictures. I can't even take a piss in the bathroom here without checking the stalls."

"I didn't realize one photo would create such interest," Binky said. "This is really great."

"Great? Listen, you jerk. You may like the thought of being hounded by these creeps, but I don't. I like my privacy."

Before Binky could reply they were interrupted by a soft knock on the door.

"What?" Dunbar yelled.

His secretary opened the door and stuck her head in the room. "Sorry, Mr. Dunbar, but there's a Ms. Lysanne and a Ms. Devereaux waiting to see you."

"Shit. Show them in, Denise. We might as well make a party out of this."

The door opened, and two women stepped past Denise and walked confidently toward the two men. The look Yemaya gave Binky sent chills down his back. She removed the envelope from his hands and pulled out the photos. After giving them a cursory glance, she handed them to Dakota.

"It looks like he's trying to pawn off some more fakes."

Dakota glanced at the pictures and smirked. "This doesn't even look like you. I can't believe Dunbar was taken in by the first ones." She sneered and tossed the photos on the editor's desk.

"Hey, those are real," Binky said.

"Yeah, right," said Dakota. "And just when were these taken?"

"Today. A few hours ago."

"Interesting. Well, not to burst your bubble, but Ms. Lysanne and I were in meetings with several newspaper editors all day...well-known and respected editors. I'd be happy to have them confirm this if you want." The glance she gave Dunbar spoke volumes. "So you see, if these were taken today, it couldn't be us."

"These are you two. You're just trying to pull something." Binky looked at Dunbar for support.

"Not at all," Yemaya said. "I can assure you that the photos you took today and the ones this newspaper published are not of us. Neither Ms. Devereaux nor I have ever been in that park. In fact, we weren't even in town the day you snapped the other picture."

Turning toward Dunbar, who had been sitting quietly through the discussion, she placed her hands, palms down, on the desk and leaned toward him. Icy, pale blue eyes burned ominously.

"Mr. Dunbar, I have no idea what you paid this man for that picture, but one thing I do know, and can prove beyond a shadow of a doubt, is that those women in the photo are not us. That means you and your paper are liable for defamation. You have two choices. You can print a front-page retraction, or my attorney will be in contact with your attorney tomorrow morning."

Dunbar snorted. "I'm not afraid of you. I've taken on bigger fish—"

"Then you're a fool," Dakota said.

"I'd be a fool to let two bitches try to threaten me. This comes under freedom of the press, and I know how to use it to my advantage."

Binky opened his mouth. Yemaya turned her gaze on him. Flinching, he snapped his jaw shut, looked away, and swallowed loudly.

Dakota noticed the change in Yemaya's expression and knew Dunbar was in trouble if she didn't do something fast.

"Mr. Dunbar. Perhaps, before you put any more of your foot in your mouth, you should give your boss a call."

"I don't need to talk to him. I have full autonomy in my job."

"Had," Yemaya growled, struggling to control the *beast* raging inside of her.

"Huh?"

"Had, Mr. Dunbar. I had a very interesting conversation with Larry Smilax about an hour ago. He likes his privacy more than you do, and he is not so anxious to go to court over this, especially after he confirmed what I've just told you."

"Hey," Binky said, "something stinks here. How'd you know about the photos if it wasn't you?"

"I guess we have the same anonymous source." Yemaya gave him an almost evil smile.

"You set me up."

Yemaya's smile widened, and then she turned back to Dunbar. "I suggest you call your boss and talk to him. Afterward, you can call my attorney and go over exactly what you will be saying in your retraction. And, just in case you believe you can intimidate me the way you have others in the past, I suggest you reconsider. You would be wise to remember I specialize in making things disappear. I doubt if too many hearts would be broken if you were one of those things."

Dunbar sputtered noisily. Yemaya straightened up and turned to look at Binky. "As for you, you need to find another occupation. Once Mr. Dunbar prints the retraction and the details of you pawning fake photos, I doubt anyone is going to want your services."

She took Dakota's arm, escorted her toward the door, and opened it. "And, Mr. Dunbar, you and your friends—if you have any—and your family might as well get used to those photographers outside. They're going to be around for a very long time. Maybe it will make you think twice before you put someone else through the same type of misery."

Dakota laughed softly at the sour expression on the editor's face.

"You might want to get a refund from Binky, here," she said. "No reason for him to profit from all of this."

Dunbar's glare was enough to tell Binky he was in big trouble. Satisfied, Yemaya and Dakota left.

"I can't believe you threatened him," Dakota whispered.

"It wasn't a threat. Just an observation."

"Yeah, right. Do you think he'll try anything?"

"No. Men like him are cowards. Besides, he likes his job too much to ignore his boss, and for all his arrogance and blustering, Dunbar isn't a stupid man."

"I'm not so sure about that, but I'll take your word for it. So what now?"

"I was thinking," Yemaya said, raising one eyebrow and smiling smugly "There is a certain hotel not far from here that is still holding three days of reservations in my name. How about we go pack our bags and make use of those rooms? We might as well get our money's worth."

"Works for me," Dakota agreed happily.

* * *

Hours later, Yemaya and Dakota arrived at the hotel, luggage in hand. Scamper was at the counter going over the list of customers and the next day's schedule.

"Ms. Lysanne, Ms. Devereaux, I wasn't sure you were coming back."

"And waste all that effort you put into making those room changes?" Yemaya said.

"Well, things happen. I can always cancel them."

"No need, Scamp. We have decided to stay here a few more days and take advantage of your kindness."

"That's wonderful! Oh, a package arrived for you yesterday. I wasn't sure what you wanted me to do with it, so I held on to it."

"A package?"

"Yeah. It's from the, um, you know, the shop I recommended."

Yemaya looked at Dakota and lowered her voice. "This should be interesting."

Once in their room, Dakota unwrapped the package and opened the box. Inside was a bottle of warming massage oil, a DVD called "Lip Service, the Cunnilingist's Guide to Stroking," and a small finger vibrator, batteries not included. Searching frantically though the box, Dakota couldn't find anything else.

"Can you believe this? No batteries. You'd think they'd buy batteries." She slammed the empty box on the bed.

"Batteries?"

"Yeah. Vibrators don't work without batteries, you know?"

"So who needs a vibrator?" Yemaya walked over to the bed and pushed Dakota backward.

"Uh..."

"Uh?"

"Uh, well," Swallowing hard, Dakota stared into the bluest eyes she had ever seen.

"Maybe I need to refresh your memory."

"Um."

Leaning down, Yemaya placed her lips next to Dakota's right ear and exhaled softly. Dakota shivered.

"Cold?" Yemaya whispered, her voice low and husky.

"I, uh..."

Laughing, Yemaya pushed herself off the bed and slowly undressed, her eyes burning with desire. When she removed her bra and panties, Dakota jumped up and tore off her own tee-shirt, pants, and underwear. She tackled Yemaya, and they both fell on the bed and broke into giggles.

"Do you think they have hidden cameras in the room?" Dakota asked teasingly, glancing at the red light glowing on the smoke detector. "I've always been suspicious of those things."

"If they do, they are about to get the show of their lives." Yemaya bared her teeth in an animal-like grin. Stretching her long body over Dakota's, she straddled her lover and lowered her breasts and stomach until the two bodies barely touched.

151

Yemaya sliding up and down against her a few times was more than enough to make Dakota gasp. Her skin tingled from the slow caresses of the nipples gliding gently across her skin. Already she could feel the wetness building between her thighs, and she squirmed.

Yemaya smiled her satisfaction and pressed her body firmly against her lover. "Anything special you want?" she whispered softly.

Dakota swallowed hard and nodded. "Yo... you."

Yemaya's eyes narrowed. She was more than satisfied with the response. Nipping Dakota's neck playfully, she proceeded to work her way down her lover's throat, then sucked at the pulse at the base of her neck. Feeling Dakota shiver, she moved slowly to her breasts. Tugging gently on the left nipple with her teeth, her low growl turned into a soft purr when Dakota groaned.

Yemaya slid farther down, her wet tongue making its way toward the blonde curls several inches below the slightly rounded stomach. Placing her cheek on the warm, soft belly, she rubbed her cheek back and forth, luxuriating in the feel of the satiny skin.

This is paradise, she thought, anticipating the next few hours of lovemaking.

Although Dakota couldn't read her partner's thoughts, she wouldn't have been surprised to know they mirrored hers. Shifting slightly, she stroked the dark head resting on her stomach and inhaled deeply. Her eyes closed in anticipation of her lover's next move. Yemaya suddenly sat up and looked around the room.

"What now?" She growled, focusing her gaze to the left side of the bed. The *beast* inside her stirred nervously and huddled in the dark recesses of its lair. It wasn't happy. Neither was Yemaya.

Dakota stared at the empty spot and frowned. "Are you okay?"

152

"I was." Yemaya glanced apologetically at Dakota and then back at the same spot. "Well. Do you need something, or do you just want to watch?"

Frowning, Dakota wasn't sure what to do or say next. The problem was quickly resolved when a white, ghostly figure shimmered into existence in front of them.

"Eeeek!" Dakota squealed and jumped backward. She grabbed the sheet and pulled it over her naked body.

"I apologize for the intrusion," the apparition said. "I needed to talk to you before I move on."

"You could have picked a better time," Dakota said.

"I didn't pick the time. It picked me."

"What does that—"

"I know you." Yemaya interrupted Dakota while closely examining her uninvited guest.

"Yes, we've met before."

Yemaya frowned. "In the sarcophagus. You were there with me."

It was Saira's turn to frown. During her visit with them in the spirit world, she had explained all of this. Perhaps their transition back to the mortal world had affected their memories. That would explain why she felt the need to return to them again. If they had forgotten their previous encounter, Yemaya would still feel uncomfortable not knowing what had happened during her illusion.

Saira nodded. "I almost cost you your life."

Dakota looked from the apparition to Yemaya and then back again.

"I felt you," Yemaya said.

"I distracted you. The air ran out before you could regain your concentration."

"Excuuuse me," Dakota said. "Am I missing something here?"

"Who are you?" Yemaya asked, ignoring Dakota.

"My name is Saira."

153

"Saira," she repeated. "And what are you?"

Saira shrugged. Even she wasn't sure exactly what she was. A few of those sensitive enough to feel her presence thought she was a ghost or energy left behind by some unhappy mortal. Others believed she was from another plane of existence or an alien.

Picking up on Dakota's thoughts, Saira chuckled. Humans were enamored with the concept of ghosts. One day, someone would discover what they really were and mankind would never be the same.

"I'm not sure there's an answer to your question. I am what I am, just as you are what you are."

Yemaya nodded her understanding. Some questions didn't have easy answers. Somehow, she knew Saira was referring to the *beast* inside her.

Mari is right about her, Saira thought. *She is special... even more so than I first imagined.* "Anyway, I came to explain what happened to you."

Saira again described how her appearance had unintentionally disrupted the balance in Yemaya's time string.

Without waiting for their response, she began to fade away.

"I must leave now. Time calls me. I wanted to apologize for disrupting your life. I never realized the effect my presence could have on mortals."

"An apology wasn't necessary. It gave Dakota and me a chance to take a much-needed vacation."

"Good. Then we'll leave it at that. Until the next time."

Saira vanished as quickly as she had appeared.

"Would you mind telling me what just happened?" Dakota wanted to pinch herself to see if she'd been dreaming.

"Now?"

"Now."

Laughing, Yemaya wrapped her arms around Dakota and pulled her close. "Okay...But this does not bode well for our relationship."

"What?" Dakota gave her a questioning look.

"Choosing talk over mad, passionate love. It sounds to me like the honeymoon is over."

Dakota snorted. "Not in this lifetime or the next. Now, quit stalling and start talking."

Leaning back, Yemaya pulled Dakota on top of her and proceeded to tell her about the incident in the sarcophagus. Seeing Saira had brought back the memories of what had happened. There would still be unanswered questions, but she was confident that between the two of them, they could come up with some reasonable conclusions.

* * *

Mari and Maopa were relieved to see their descendants happily curled up in bed. Mari waved her hand across the Eternal Flame, and the images of the two women vanished.

"Looks like thangs turned out jest fine."

"A good thing too, but we're still going to have some explaining to do once they get back to normal."

"Yep. They shore gonna be surprised when Tommy brings them newest toys we done ordered. It's a dern shame we can't get him ta deliver 'em here," Maopa said sorrowfully.

"Let's make our own," Mari said. "After all, we're spirits. We can do anything we want here."

A slight cough distracted them.

"If you'll excuse me, I think I have other things to attend to." Before either could answer, Intunecat disappeared.

"I'll be danged. I ain't never seen a spirit blush quite like that 'afore."

"Neither have I," Mari said with a laugh. She took Maopa by the hand and the two spirits vanished, each mentally designing what they hoped would be the ultimate toy.

CHAPTER 2 5

UNWILLING TO INTRUDE on her father during one of his infamous orgies, the Child waited until all of Dis' guests and sycophants departed. Only then did she walk boldly into his abode, ignoring the furtive looks of the minions who faithfully served him.

"So," bellowed the Underlord, eyeing his daughter appreciatively. "Have you finally cut the apron strings to your mother?"

"There were no strings, Father. Mother and I have an understanding."

"An understanding. How civilized. Why are you here? Are we to have an *understanding*?"

"We understand each other quite well."

Dis laughed. She was definitely his daughter, a fact that made him proud and wary. The blood in her veins ran hot with power. That was more than enough to make her a capable adversary. With his sibling's blood also in her veins through Lilith, her unique lineage provided a potent mixture of two of the most powerful beings in existence.

Had Caelene been anyone else but his daughter, Dis would have destroyed her immediately, ridding himself of a serious rival. Instead, he was curious. Curious about her plans to dethrone him, which he was well aware of, and curious about his own feelings for her. He had many offspring, but none stirred his emotions like the Child. Then again, none of his wives had held his attention or affection like Lilith.

Like mother, like child, he mused silently before replying to her statement. "Yes, I believe we do," he said, motioning for Caelene to sit. "I'm sure this isn't a daughterly visit. What can I do for you?"

He poured one of his favorite drinks, a cold soda, and handed it to her.

"You can be so human," she said, indicating the beverage.

"I can be a lot of things when I want."

"A warning, Father?"

"Why would I need to warn you of anything?"

"Why indeed," Caelene said, enjoying the verbal exchange.

Dis sat down across from her, crossed his legs, and relaxed against the backrest. His brightly polished burgundy hooves glistened, reflecting the dancing flames from within the fireplace. Reaching down, he flicked a small object off his right hoof.

"It's so hard to get good help these days," he said absent-mindedly. "You'd think after all this time my staff would be able to keep this place clean."

Caelene shrugged. "You want the impossible. The Underworld isn't any different than other realms."

"Ah. The voice of experience. And just how much traveling have you done since your release?"

"You're getting old, Father. You forget that I spent an eternity observing worlds."

"I don't forget anything Daughter, but observation isn't the same as experience. Now, why are you here?"

"And I was just beginning to enjoy this little chat. Perhaps another time. I want to talk to the Twin."

Dis's chocolate brown eyes gave no indication of his thoughts. If the Child had been able to read his mind, she would have had the satisfaction of knowing she had jolted him from his normal complacency.

"Why?" he asked, his deep baritone voice indicating nothing more than curiosity.

"That's my business."

"I see. Then I guess this little *chat* is over."

Caelene expected her father to show more curiosity. His abrupt refusal stunned her. She knew if she left now, the topic could never be broached again.

Dis watched his daughter's face. Although she appeared stoic, he was a master at reading expressions.

"I have questions," the Child blurted out and then bit her lower lip, regretting the momentary loss of control.

Dis smiled. *So old and still a child. But a dangerous one.* "What questions? Perhaps I can answer them."

"You can't."

"Can't. How can you be so sure?"

Caelene hesitated. It was true he probably could, but she wanted more. She wanted to meet the Twin, the creator of her mother...to understand what type of person he was...to know the uncle whose blood ran through her veins.

"Maybe you could answer some, but you can't give me the one thing he can."

"Which is?"

"The personal experience. The one-on-one, face-to-face feeling of meeting someone for the first time."

"That's it? You simply want the *experience*?"

"That's it," Caelene said, aware that her father wasn't fooled by her lie.

"But what if he doesn't want to meet you? I don't imagine you're one of his most favorite people, even if you are kin."

"I'm not asking permission, Father. I just want to know *how* to reach him. I can take care of the rest."

Dis threw back his head and laughed. The sound carried to all the corners of the Underworld, causing its inhabitants to stop what they were doing and listen. It was rare that anything amused their master to that extent.

"You certainly have courage, I'll give you that. But I can't help you. Even if I told you, no one sees him unless he wants them to...well, except me," Dis said, smirking. "Blood trumps blood." The Child thought about those three words and smiled. Perhaps that was the key she needed.

"Don't be so quick to assume things, Daughter. Your blood isn't pure. You would never get past the barriers, even if you knew where they were."

"Then why don't you tell me if it's so impossible?"

"I'm tempted. Watching you try might be interesting," Dis said. It certainly would stir things up in the Twin's realm.

"Will you help me?" Caelene asked hopefully.

"I'll think about it."

"When will I know?"

"When I tell you my decision and no sooner. Now, I think we have enjoyed each other's company long enough, don't you?"

Caelene knew she wasn't getting any more information. She would have to be patient or else find the path on her own.

"As you wish, Father," she said reluctantly.

Rising, she placed the glass on a nearby stand and departed, leaving Dis both amused and contemplative. Perhaps that was why he hadn't immediately noticed the arrival of another during his chat with Caelene.

"Traveler," he boomed, his voice deep and commanding. "Show yourself."

Saira complied immediately, although not intimidated by the Underlord. It was more out of respect for First Born. As powerful as Dis was, he held no power over her.

"Underlord," she said, tipping her head to acknowledge his position.

"It's been a long time, Traveler. What brings you here uninvited? Surely there are others more interesting that call to you?"

"Not at the moment. I would not be here, otherwise."

Dis motioned for her to sit.

"And I wouldn't be plagued by another female. All I need now is for Lilith to show up, and my day will be perfect."

* * *

Saira had a premonition that his day was about to become even less to his liking. Once Lilith learned of her daughter's desire to meet the Twin, she would definitely want to talk to Dis. At this very moment, one of his less-than-loyal minions was scurrying off to inform her of the meeting between the Child and her father.

Dis had learned long ago that many of his followers were more fond of his ex than he. Allegiances rarely lasted forever. Still, it was amusing to let them snitch. Lilith wasn't a threat. Besides, if the news brought her back to the Underworld for the occasional visit, he didn't object. She was still the most fascinating and beautiful demoness he had ever met. Perhaps the only person he had ever truly and passionately loved.

"So, again, why are you here?"

"You and the Child being together is enough to attract a lot of attention, if it were known. How could I not follow her *thread* here?"

"Whatever happened to privacy? As supreme ruler of this realm, I, at least, could have some."

"One would think," Saira agreed, smiling slightly. The Child was right. Dis seemed so human at times. "I apologize for the intrusion. You know how I am."

"Yes, yes. We've done this before. I guess I should be happy that Lilith was your last attraction. Otherwise, I fear I would be plagued by your visits more often. Do you still not consume food and liquids?" he asked unexpectedly.

Surprised at the sudden change of topic, Saira shook her head. "Time changes many things, but that's one thing that even it can't alter. I sometimes wish I could sample such things as food and liquid. Then I might understand your cravings for such human things as sodas."

Dis smirked. "A small weakness. Nothing more."

"But a huge confession. An Underlord isn't supposed to have weaknesses."

"Everything has weaknesses. I just happen to have fewer than the rest."

"Except the Twin."

Dis' lips curved upward into a wry grin.

"He isn't perfect, contrary to what some believe. His failed experiments prove that."

"You mean like humanity. Had you not interfered it could have ended differently."

"My interference occurred only after it went wrong. Lilith had evolved well beyond his expectations. She'd never have survived in the stagnant world he created."

"Are you so sure, Underlord? She may have helped Adam evolve faster. He suffered his own growing pains."

"True. My twin wanted her returned for that reason. He knew she was necessary to complete his experiment. She exceeded even his expectations. I believe he thought Adam would catch up."

"He would have," Saira said.

"But at what cost to her? How long was she expected to wait?"

"You sound so sanctimonious. Surely you don't want me to believe your reasons for abducting her were pure?"

"Pure?" Dis threw back his head and roared his laughter. "Of course they were. Pure lust. Pure envy. Pure desire. I coveted her. And I enjoyed messing with his mind. Taking

Lilith satisfied everything I wanted. She was perfect. Beautiful, intelligent, innocent. An irresistible combination."

"Only it backfired, didn't it? She grew to know you better than you expected. You're lucky she never wanted your throne."

"That was never a possibility," Dis replied. "Like I said, she was perfect. Ambition has never been part of Lilith."

"Unlike the Child."

The remark brought Dis' thoughts back to Caelene's visit.

"My daughter has more of my traits than her mother's."

"Are you worried?"

Dis shrugged. "All things come to an end. One of my blood would be the logical replacement. She would be my choice. It's unlikely it will happen soon, though."

"What about her wish to meet the Twin? Are you going to help her?"

"She's within her rights to demand it, but it's not within my power to grant such a meeting. Only he can do that."

"But you can show her the way."

"If I choose to."

"Then I'm done here," Saira said, rising from her chair.

Dis nodded. "I've enjoyed our conversation, Traveler. Until the next time."

"Until the next time," Saira said, and was gone.

* * *

The Child paced back and forth. Waiting was never one of her outstanding qualities, even though she had spent an eternity trapped in the Netherworld. If Father didn't give her an answer soon, she'd have no choice but to search for the path on her own.

"I see patience isn't one of your strong points," Dis said, walking in unannounced.

"And knocking isn't one of yours."

"Like daughter, like father."

162

Caelene couldn't argue the point so she ignored the comment. "Have you made your decision?"

"Yes, although your mother isn't going to like it."

"Mother has nothing to do with this."

"Lilith will think differently. You make sure she knows this is your idea. I don't want that spitfire nagging me for the next thousand years."

"Please, Father. Don't tell me you're afraid of her."

"Not afraid, but trust me, Lilith is one person no one should cross. She's more than capable of making my life pure hell."

Caelene snorted. Dis wasn't exaggerating.

"If Mother finds out, I'll tell her I forced you to help me."

It was Dis' turn to snort. Then he gave Caelene precise directions to the gate of the Overworld.

"Remember, you may make it to the gate, but that doesn't guarantee entry. Only my twin can let you in."

"What about you?"

"I don't need a gateway. As twins, we have a connection that prevents exclusion. He considers it a curse." Dis laughed. "I think it's a great way to annoy him. Dropping in uninvited frustrates him."

"I know the feeling," the Child said.

"So do I," Dis replied. "It's getting to be a habit down here."

"Point taken, Father. Next time I'll announce myself."

"Make certain you do. My patience is very limited."

The stern look he gave her was enough to tell the Child that he was serious. Dis had mellowed over the ages, but was more powerful than ever. He had learned to control his anger. Now he focused only on those things that were real threats to him or his domain. There weren't many. The Underworld was like a well-oiled machine. Each minion or demon knew his or her place and what was expected of them, and Dis overlooked the mischief-making.

The path to the gate was complicated. Only Dis' precise instructions enabled the Child to reach the gate to the Overworld. Caeline was surprised when no one challenged her at the entrance.

The enormous arch glistened, rays of blinding golden light illuminating everything as far as the eye could see. Shadows moved quickly in and out giving the impression that the entrance was only an illusion.

Caelene touched the invisible barrier with her fingertips and was immediately thrown backward. Stunned, she approached it again, leaning forward to examine the entrance. When she saw nothing, she hesitantly touched it again, only to find herself once more on her butt several feet away.

"I won't give up," she said aloud.

"You'll never be allowed to enter," a deep voice replied. "Go home."

The Child recognized the voice. It reminded her of Dis.

"I've come to talk to you."

"What made you think I'd talk to you, Child? You've done enough damage." Caelene was surprised that the Twin spoke so bluntly, but without animosity. She had been sure he would be angry with her for corrupting Eve.

"That was a long time ago," she said. "I've changed."

"Have you?"

His laughter made her uncomfortable. She felt as if it were Dis.

"Yes. I'm older and wiser."

"And more ambitious. My brother needs to watch you more closely, but that's not my problem. What brings you here?"

"I wanted to meet my mother's creator. I'm entitled to at least that."

"You're entitled to nothing from me. I had nothing to do with your conception. Lilith made her choice. Once she left here, I was no longer responsible for her or her offspring."

"You created her. You can't simply discard her as if she never existed. If Mother didn't turn out like you wanted, then your experiment failed. She can't be blamed for that."

"Go home, little girl." For the first time the Voice sounded angry. "I don't have time to mince words with the likes of you."

It was Caelene's turn to laugh.

"The likes of me? What are you so afraid of, uncle? Am I a reminder that you aren't perfect? That you are flawed like the rest of us. Or am I taking you away from another experiment? Surely you can spare a few moments for your own niece. Aren't you the least curious about me? After all, your tinkering is what made me possible."

"Do you think your petty efforts will now get you what you want? I know what you're trying to do and it won't work. Now go away before I'm forced to send you back to the Underworld."

"Do it! I'll just come back. I've already spent an eternity in the Netherworld. What's another one here?" The Voice didn't respond. "Eventually you'll have to talk to me," Caelene insisted.

"You ruined one of my greatest experiments," the Voice finally said.

The Child snorted. "It was ruined before I was born. Mother's actions proved that."

"Thanks to my brother. Had he not interfered, my children would still be here."

"Children? They were your creations, not your offspring. Besides, Mother was already unhappy before Father took her."

"She would have adjusted."

"Mother would never have *adjusted* as you so quaintly put it. She wanted to be Adam's equal. You denied her that."

"In time she would have received it."

The lack of emotion in his tone told Caelene that the Twin was growing bored with the conversation.

"In time? She should have been equal the moment you made them. All she asked was that Adam treat her that way."

"Adam needed time. She could have been more patient. I'd have given her what she wanted, eventually."

"Eventually wasn't good enough. She asked so little of you. You failed her. You failed them and humanity," the Child said boldly.

"And when did you become humanity's champion?" the Twin asked. "Your interference was what caused their banishment. If you'd minded your own business, my chil...my creations would have been happy."

You don't get it, Caelene thought. "No, they wouldn't. You created a perfect world with imperfect inhabitants. It was doomed to fail."

"We'll never know for sure, will we?" the Voice said. The Child knew he was right. "So, now we're at an impasse. Go home, child. Maybe in time I will listen to your ramblings."

Furious at his dismissal, Caelene was about to respond when she suddenly found herself back in her living room in the Underworld. Dis was standing in front of the fireplace. Caelene started to speak, but he held up his hand.

"Wait," he said.

Although she wanted to rebel, her instincts told her to obey. The Underlord nodded his approval and then looked past her right shoulder. Within seconds, the air shimmered and Saira appeared.

"I knew you couldn't resist this meeting," Dis said.

"You're beginning to know me too well, Underlord," Saira replied. "How are you, Caelene?" She moved to stand next to the small demoness.

"Great! An audience."

"I suggest you get used to it." Dis grinned, almost sympathetically. "How was your little visit with my twin?"

"Pfffft! I would have been better off not meeting him. My expectations were greater than the reality."

"Aren't they always?" Saira said.

"He talked to me like I was a child."

166

The slight stamp of her small hoof amused Dis, but he knew better than to remark on it. "He does the same thing to me," he said. "You'd think he was the elder."

"I thought he was. Everyone thinks he is," Caelene said.

"Everyone may be right. Neither of us knows for sure. Personally, it makes no difference to me. I claim that I'm the elder to irritate him. It appears he has someone else who can do that now." Dis laughed.

"No one treats me like he did," Caelene declared. "If he thinks sending me back here is going to stop me, he's got another thought coming."

"Leave it alone, Daughter."

"You doubt my ability or will?"

"No. I know my twin. You're not a match for him...yet."

"Is this wise?" Saira asked.

"Wise, Traveler?" Dis thought about it for a few moments. "Perhaps not, but wisdom and truth can take different paths. You, better than anyone, know this."

"I know that you're playing a dangerous game. One that may have bigger consequences than even you can imagine."

The Underlord shrugged. "You know me. I never plan for the future. Today is all that matters, and today isn't the right time for the Child to test her powers."

"You talk about me as if I didn't exist," Caelene said angrily. "I will not be treated like a child by you either."

"Then don't act like one," Dis replied. "I may be your father, but more important, I'm your master. You will do as I say, or I'll send you back to the Netherworld. Do we understand each other, Caelene?"

The use of her real name by Dis surprised her, but his eyes spoke volumes. The fires of hell burned brightly in the chocolate brown gaze. Before her stood the real Underlord, lord and master of his domain. Only once before had she aroused his wrath, and she paid dearly for it. Caelene bowed her head. "As you command...sire." The words left a bitter taste in her mouth.

"Good." He nodded his approval, knowing it galled her to be submissive. "There's hope for you, yet." Turning his back toward the Child, he winked at Saira and then once again assumed the serious, stoic face of supreme ruler. "If you two will excuse me, I have more important matters to attend to. My guests are waiting."

He strolled to the door and looked once more toward Caelene. "You may be of my blood, but don't make the mistake of thinking it gives you any advantages. I'm aware of your powers, Child, just as you are aware of mine. Disobey me, and I'll destroy you. Even my fondness for your mother won't stop me. Do I make myself clear?"

"Perfectly." Caelene's eyes flashed rebelliously.

The Underlord stepped through the door and left.

"Arrogant bastard," Caelene said.

The booming laughter from beyond the room made it clear he had heard her.

Saira watched in amusement while the demoness paced back and forth. As a child, Caelene had experienced the unforgiving wrath of the Underlord. As an adult, he made sure she remembered the lesson.

"This isn't over," she said.

"I don't imagine it is."

Glancing at Saira, Caelene frowned. "Have you ever met the Twin?"

"No. I can't find a good *thread*."

"And yet you found Father's."

"The Underlord has never been reclusive. He enjoys life too much. Many *threads* lead to him."

"Surely his must connect to his brother."

"They do, but they stop at the gate to the Overworld."

"How can that be? Time has no barriers. There's no physicality to it. Besides, Father doesn't have any problems crossing the gateway."

"They have the same blood. That has nothing to do with the *threads*."

"Well, there has to be another way through the gate. I'll find it."

"I believe you," Saira said, and she did. Interesting times were ahead. "When that moment comes, I'll be watching."

"I'm beginning to understand Father's frustrations," Caelene said. "Having you drop in uninvit—"

Before she could finish her sentence, Saira was gone.

"Hell! I'm beginning to appreciate humans more and more. At least they have an excuse for their rudeness."

Caelene walked to a small red cabinet near the fireplace, opened its door, and peered inside. Several shelves held shiny red cans covered with a thin layer of frost. She grabbed one, closed the door, and sat down in her favorite chair. After popping the top, she took a few sips and leaned back, staring at the label.

"Like father, like daughter," she said and then giggled. Contrary to the way it seemed at times, the Child looked forward to an interesting and exciting future.

* * *

Saira touched the familiar *thread* and smiled. It was only a matter of time before she returned to see where it ended. Until then, the present would await her return, for already the past called with a compelling tug.

The End

About The Author

FRAN HECKROTTE lives in the Sunny South with her husband, her dogs, fish chickens, goose and duck. Her life experiences include living in Alaska, gold panning, bull riding, scuba diving, flying, training gaited horses and more. After spending five years in law enforcement, she switched to construction and eventually opened her own property management company. Favorite town is Montréal. Hobbies include gardening, beaches, skiing, photography and reading. Feel free to email her at franheck@hotmail.com.

About the Copy Editor

CINDY BURKE has had a lifelong interest in journalism and fiction writing. She started as a newsroom assistant and has contributed several articles to local newspapers. Her science fiction book, "Intimate Space: A Feminist Utopian Romp Through the Galaxy," was published in 2015.

Burke is a social justice advocate and member of the Clemson Alumni Society for Equality (CASE), an alumni group that supports LGBTQIA initiatives. She can be reached at CindyBurke.com.

Her family is spread across the Southeast, including two sons, a sous chef and a navy technician. Burke lives with her husband, a computer analyst and fellow sci-fi and fantasy buff, in the foothills of the beautiful Blue Ridge Mountains.

About the Cover Artist

PATTY G. HENDERSON is an author, publisher and artist and all around bohemian at heart. An independent author, she launched her own publishing imprint, Blanca Rosa Publishing. She writes Gothic Historical Romances and has published four so far, THE SECRET OF LIGHTHOUSE POINTE, CASTLE OF

DARK SHADOWS, PASSION FOR VENGEANCE, and SHADOWS OF THE HEART. She has also penned four Brenda Strange Supernatural Mysteries,

Comfortable wearing several creative hats, Patty is an accomplished artist as well as author. She's done popular book cover artwork for many mainstream mystery and horror authors and lesbian authors via her graphic arts business, Boulevard Photografica, in addition to a nearly complete immersion in indie writing and publishing.

You can reach Patty via her author web site: www.pattyghenderson.com or check out her graphics and book cover professional web site: www.boulevardphotografica.yolasite.com.

Other Titles by Fran Heckrotte

The Illusionist (First in the Illusionist Series)

DAKOTA DEVEREAUX, an investigative journalist, is on a mission to uncover the secrets of Yemaya, the Illusionist. However, in her quest for an exposé on this mysterious woman, she uncovers more than she bargained for. Dakota is targeted by a power hungry CEO determined to learn the Illusionist's secret at all costs, and a madman intent on fulfilling his perverted fantasies.

From Moldova, land of the legendary werewolf, to the Transylvania and the Carpathian Mountains, two souls must battle the dark forces of evil for their lives and their love.

Bloodlust (Second in the Illusionist Series)

YEMAYA AND DAKOTA have just returned to the Illusionist's homeland for a well-earned vacation when they are informed that several villagers have been savagely attacked and killed by something or someone.

At the same time, a young Carpi woman is found lying unconscious near the outskirts of Teraclia. Comatose, she is unable to tell anyone what has happened and science can provide no answers. Two small wounds on her throat raise the old specter of the vampire, a legend the locals of the Transylvanian community are very familiar with and still believe to this day.

The Illusionist and her partner search for the truth behind these attacks. Will they fall prey to the murderous bloodlust that surrounds them, or will they succeed in stopping this heinous reign of terror?

Lilith (Third in the Illusionist Series)

YEMAYA, the Illusionist, and her journalist partner, Dakota, find themselves embroiled in a search for the person responsible for the rape and torture of a young Carpi woman attending a university in the States.

When they decide to visit a local nightclub for "women only," they find the owner and her employees unusual. Dakota feels mysteriously attracted to one of the clientele while Yemaya recognizes a kindred spirit in Lilith, the club's owner. Spiritual ancestors, missing whores, a sadistic exporter and new acquaintances lead the two lovers into an adventure of Biblical proportion.

Lilith! She was a demoness, as old as humanity itself. Now she is the owner of a "women's only" nightclub and part owner of the Sisterhood, a small group of whores who have banded together to create a better life for themselves. It is her job to protect the women who are putting so much trust in her.

When a local pimp decides to eliminate his competition, Lilith and her two demon partners want revenge and no one knows better how to exact it than demons. This is a revelation of the past, the present and the events that forever changed the course of human history.

Les Gris, The Shadow People (Fourth in the Illusionist Series)

THEY WERE LES GRIS, the Shadow People, and they are as much a part of us as we are them. As children we talked to them, played with them and disclosed our innermost fears, secrets and dreams; they patiently listened, comforted and encouraged us.

In time, though, most humans outgrew their *imaginary* friends and eventually forgot them. For those few who didn't, humanity's very existence would be determined by the strength

---

of the bond between a small group of women and their life partners, the *les gris*.

Saira (Fifth in the Illusionist Series)

SAIRA WAS A TRAVELER. Even her name meant 'traveler'. Her entire existence was dedicated to making the journey to seek answers to the questions that plagued her. Sometimes she felt as if she were a pawn in a game she didn't understand but knew her destiny was hers to decide. She chose to let the uncertainty of time make the decisions for her.

Unfortunately, her curiosity not only gets her into trouble but creates a series of events that affects not only the mortal world but the spirit world too. Yemaya, Dakota, Mari and Maopa will find their lives turned topsy-turvy and Saira will learn an emotion she had never experienced before...fear.

Warrior Demoness (Sixth in the Illusionist Series)

SHE WAS SABNOCK, a demon, who, like the Phoenix, lived and died many times because she chose to live amongst mortals rather than spend eternity babysitting the legions of the Underlord.

There were no longer battles to be fought in the Underworld so the ex-commander left her realm to live with the humans as a human. Falling in love, she now had to choose between her vow to live and die as a mortal or love and live as a demon, not knowing if her lover could accept the truth. The wrong decision would condemn her to a life of loneliness—and for a demon, life was eternity.

Solaria (Futuristic Science Fiction)

THE FIRST AWARENESS of existence was a chaotic flash of colors, meaningless and yet in an odd way logical. Why, she isn't sure. Birth is the most significant event in life, and yet it is never memorable, at least not for the newborn.

But then, she really isn't a newborn, even though it is the first day of her life. She is 1A526, the first of her kind, an artificially intelligent blend of technology and bio-mechanics. Created to serve humans, Solaria and her AI programmer, Carley, soon discover the company funding the Hubot Project has more sinister motives.

If Solaria is to fulfill the hopes of the woman who gave her existence meaning, she has to become the human her programmer dreamed of and take down Future Dynamicon, the company that created her.

Future Perfect (Sequel to Solaria)

PRIMERIS WAS a Hubot, designed to serve humans. Her existence depended on her ability to complete her assignments...which she always did with a cold, emotionless detachment. Now, her perfect record is going to be tested to its limits. In her attempts to find and capture Solaria, another Hubot, Primeris is forced to either disobey her directive of obedience or become the human she never wanted to be.

The Order of the Healers was exactly that, healers. Their mission was to move humanity forward, even if it meant saving the worst of mankind. Chantelle is a Singer, a member of a small sub-group of Healers, whose latest calling takes her on a mission that will test her gift to its limit, and leave her wondering if her success will lead to humanity's downfall.

Rapture, Sins of the Sinners
By A.C. Henley and Fran Heckrotte

THERE'S A SERIAL killer running rampant in the state of Texas and she's not yet quenched her thirst for blood. Practiced in her craft, she is good with a blade and leaves no trace behind.

When a pattern becomes evident in murders in Ft. Worth, savvy detective Agnes Kelly-Elliott is assigned to the case. With her partner Jeff, Agnes quickly starts to work to solve the murders happening in her district.

From all across the state and with no apparent end in sight, Texas Ranger Cochetta Lovejoy is certain she knows just who this killer might be. She relentlessly pursues her suspect and, when she meets up with her, sets in motion events which can never be undone.

Odyssey of the Butterfly

TAKE A JOURNEY through space, time and the imagination....all with a common thread, butterflies. If you like science fiction, fantasy, zombies or romance, these five short stories offer a little of each, and more. Can you solve the mystery of the butterfly or will it leave you wondering the next time you see one flitting by?